MONDO MARILYN

Other books by
Richard Peabody & Lucinda Ebersole:

MONDO ELVIS
MONDO BARBIE

MONDO Marilyn

Edited by

Lucinda Ebersole

&

Richard Peabody

St. Martin's Press / New York

Design by Jaye Zimet

ISBN 0-312-11853-8

First Edition: February 1995
10 9 8 7 6 5 4 3 2 1

For Carmen Delzell and Steven Ford Brown
—R.P.

For Camille and Madonna
—L.E.

Special thanks to: Ann Acosta, Diane Apostolos-Cappadona, Herman Ayayo, Harriet Barlow, Kevin Bezner, Ann Burrola, John Clark, Nita Congress, Charis Conn, Denise Duhamel, Susie Earley, Leona Fisher, Bob and Kitty Gillman, Kate Glahn, Alex Gram, Richard Grayson, David Greisman, A. M. Homes, Derrick Hsu, Keith Kahla, Ken Louden, Fiona Mackintosh, Beth Milleman, Glenn Moomau, F. R. Nagle, Paul Pasquarella, Beverly Cleghorn Ricks, Beth Schneiderman, Janie Sheppard, David and Lynn Sheridan, Brian Sheridan, Julia Slavin, Allan and Kim Stypeck, Henry Taylor, Nancy Taylor, Alice K. Turner, Tom Whalen, and Reva Wolf.

Contents

For beauty is no guarantee.
—Tracey Thorn

Introduction

Marilyn: Hits Like a Bombshell.
—*The Washington Post*, October 1993

Marilyn Monroe is the most legendary woman of the twentieth century. Know of any challengers? Elizabeth Taylor? Madonna? Let's take a look at a mere sampling of the Marilyn Monroe mania that exists in our collective consciousness. Please remember that this data is changing as you read this.

In the District of Columbia she watches us from a rooftop mural. There have been seventeen Marilyn Monroe plays, including ex-husband Arthur Miller's *After the Fall* and Norman Mailer's *Strawhead*, a play in which Mailer's own daughter starred. And speaking of Mailer, hasn't he made a bit of a career out of invoking Marilyn Monroe's name. His obsession is typical—he never met her.

There have been fourteen made-for-TV movies about Marilyn and seven films with Marilyn Monroe characters, including the Nicolas Roeg version of the Terry Miller play *Insignificance*. In *Insignificance*, Marilyn shows Einstein how relativity works. This film starred Roeg's wife, Theresa Russell, as Marilyn, proving that everything is relative! The rock opera *Tommy*, filmed by Ken Russell, features the famous Marilyn chapel. The visual imaging of "Marilyn the Icon" takes over our psyche.

A ballet in England in 1975 bore the clever title *Marilyn: A Ballet*. Recently an opera about Marilyn premiered. High culture found in Marilyn what more pedestrian culture had known all along. Though Marilyn's career in life centered around the movies, in her afterlife, television became a popular medium. Marilyn as character appeared as a part of the story line in such diverse programs as *I Love Lucy*, *Benson*, *M*A*S*H*, and *Matt Houston*. There has been a song or two, most notably Elton John's "Candle in the Wind." Postage stamps in Mali and the Congo. A Japanese robot Marilyn who plays guitar and sings, and if you saw Madonna's "Material Girl" on video there should have been an instant "Diamonds are a girl's best friend" flashback. For Madonna, Marilyn is a girl's best friend.

But what about the real Marilyn? Unfortunately, there is no longer a "real" Marilyn. If there were, she would be in her seventies now and most probably forgotten except by those late-night movie buffs who watch her on the TV screen. She will be forever etched in our minds as the young blond with the breathy voice and the white skirt billowing up in the air. That image of her is seared in our minds as an American icon. Everyone knows who she is, but few know who she was. She died leaving behind no Rosetta stone to guide us, and so we make it up.

The stories and poems in this collection offer a wide range of writers who have formed their own mythology about Marilyn Monroe. Clive Barker's nasty little Marilyn number peeks under the windblown skirt and reveals the horror of cinema gone splatter happy. The protagonist in Rosanne Daryl Thomas's story uses technology and plastic surgery to create a Marilyn of his own.

Hillary Johnson portrays an aging Marilyn among drag queens. Julia Dubner has her reading James Joyce, a story drawn from viewing the actual photo of Marilyn doing just that. In Judy Grahn's poem, she reclaims the fragile Marilyn by digging up her bones. Sharon Olds shows the archetypal woman done wrong by the system. Charles Bukowski and Jeanne Beaumont see her as a victim, sucked dry by the dream machine.

John Rechy's piece is one of the best of an ever-repetitive theme, Marilyn and the Kennedys. Rechy looks at the life of a woman who just may be Marilyn's daughter. Tom Whalen contributes a fantastic voyage around the body. Doris Grumbach and Sam Toperoff fictionalize the poor Norma Jean. These writers and the other writers in this collection bring a unique and compelling view to the myth that is Marilyn.

Marilyn Monroe was America's sacrifice on the sexual altar. We glorified in her flesh, in her every wiggle and sizzle. She was the epitome of sex in the repressed, uptight fifties, a harbinger of things to come. Looking up at her image that stares down at us from the rooftop in Washington, she seems tame, almost demure. In today's culture, she would probably not be a big star. She would be too heavy, too soft spoken, too sweet, but she might just be your best friend. That vulnerable, puckish personality, the desire to be loved, the wacky sense of humor might lead you to conclude that, diamonds aside, Marilyn was our best friend.

—*LUCINDA EBERSOLE*
—*RICHARD PEABODY*

For Marilyn M.

Charles Bukowski

slipping keenly into bright ashes,
target of vanilla tears
your sure body lit candles for men
on dark nights,
and now your night is darker
than the candle's reach
and we will forget you, somewhat,
and it is not kind
but real bodies are nearer
and as the worms pant for your bones,
I would so like to tell you
that this happens to bears and elephants
to tyrants and heroes and ants
and frogs,
still, you brought us something,
some type of small victory,
and for this I say: good
and let us grieve no more;
like a flower dried and thrown away,
we forget, we remember,
we wait. child, child, child,
I raise my drink a full minute
and smile.

Marilyn Monroe Comes to Rock Falls

Leslie Pietrzyk

No one would believe me if I told them, but last night I saw Marilyn Monroe come into Jack Dorry's drugstore, strike me down with lightning if I ain't telling the truth.

It was me and Dilly sitting at the counter, sharing an ice cream soda, me trying to race her to the bottom first. She started laughing—always does, got no staying power, if she were a boy and a baseball player she'd be the guy who goes in to strike out a left-handed batter. So I hit bottom while she was laughing, made that scraping sound with my straw for a good minute just to prove I was down there.

"Rafe Johnston, you're a pure embarrassment," she said. "What'm I gonna do with you?" She was only 12 years old but sounding more and more like her mother every day. All of a sudden this summer the girls were sounding like their mothers and starting to look like their older sisters, those clusters of girls that were to us nothing more than a swoop of giggles and perfume, matched sweater sets and high heels, maybe a swish of bright red lipstick.

I didn't know what to think about this. So maybe I pretended it wasn't happening.

The fat girl behind the soda counter said, "Stop that racket." Naturally I kept going, and Dilly laughed some more. Her laugh was like big round Os coming out of her mouth, one after another, bigger and bigger, rounder and rounder. I could see that laugh plain as if it were written out on paper. We'd been blood best friends near about forever.

"I'll write up a report on you," the fat girl said. She was always threatening to write up a report on you and give it to Jack Dorry so you wouldn't be allowed back in for sodas. "Swear to God this time I will."

Jack glanced up from the pharmacy counter, gave me a two-finger wave and a wink. I was clean-up batter for the Jack Dorry Drug Store Yankees Little League team and everyone said near about the best center fielder in town for my age.

Dilly pinched the straw shut with her fingers and laughed out another trail of Os as my breath got caught up inside my mouth.

It was like any other night that summer, any other night I had some money from weed-picking or mowing a lawn to treat me and Dilly.

"Excuse me, please." Not any voice we knew, so Dilly and I spun our stools around, but a big display of soap flakes on sale blocked our view. "Can you help me, please, sir?"

"Holy cow." The fat girl had moved to the far end of the counter for a look-see. She fluffed her bangs, tightened her ponytail, wiped her hands forward and back against her apron. "Hooooly cow," she whispered, forgetting to shut her mouth afterwards.

Dilly hopped off the stool and peeked around the soap flakes. "Rafe!" she called. "It's Marilyn Monroe! Right here in Rock Falls!"

It was exactly what Dilly'd pull on me, so I wasn't in any rush, but there was Jack hitching his pants over his gut and that fat girl still hadn't thought to close up her mouth, so, sure, I looked around the soap flakes, and there she was, Marilyn Monroe, and all I could think of was, There she is, there she is, and probably my mouth was swinging wide just like everyone else's, I was that afraid I'd have to talk to her.

Dilly grabbed my hand. "Will you look at her?" she whispered. "Just look."

It's not like I needed an invitation.

She wasn't saying anything, just standing stock still like it was something she had to get out of the way, this flurried excitement—that once we'd filled ourselves up with staring she could get to what she'd come in for.

Jack was heading around the pharmacy counter, and that was about as unusual as Marilyn Monroe in our drugstore, since Jack always shouted across the store if anyone needed help.

"Good evening, ma'am," he said, reaching for the top of his head like he was wearing a hat, realizing he wasn't so ending up wiping off his forehead instead.

She smiled. Marilyn smiled just for him. "Good evening. What a lovely shop you have here."

Jack bowed. Swear to God, actually bowed.

Marilyn said, "I wonder if you might be able to help me find something."

"I'd be honored, ma'am," Jack said. He was sounding a little like Gary Cooper. "What can I do for you? I'm sure we've got whatever you're looking for. Candy, gum, cigarettes, comics." Dilly and I quick looked at each other, then back, each of us thinking the same thing: Like Marilyn Monroe reads comics. Jack bit his lip.

"I was just out taking a drive," she said. She cocked her head sideways, looking like a little bird waiting to be fed.

"Lovely evening for a drive," Jack said.

She nodded. "I was wondering," and she paused, took a deep breath that seemed to fill her entire body, looked all the way around the room. She must have seen us staring at her, certainly she saw the fat girl at the counter, but she leaned in close like Jack was the only person in the store. "I was wondering," she said, and she looked around again, and leaned even closer; she put her hand on his arm, and he froze, maybe even stopped breathing. "I was wondering," and she tiptoed up to whisper something in his ear, and Lord, did his face end up red like she was breathing the color straight into his ear to his cheeks and all the way down his neck.

"Just a minute," he said—no more Gary Cooper, he could hardly get the words out.

She stepped away and looked at the floor, scuffed her shoe back and forth, rubbed her lips together, folded her arms and sighed. Jack stared at her long enough for the red to drain itself down, and then he clumped to the next aisle over.

I nudged Dilly with my elbow. "What'd she say to him?" I whispered. "What's over there?"

"Sshh," she said, same note and stretching it out the way my mother did in church.

Marilyn walked to the cash register at the pharmacy counter and pulled a single bill out of her purse, didn't even look at it as she set it on the counter.

"Probably a hundred-dollar bill," I said.

"Sshh."

Jack had something tucked in his arms, but I couldn't see, and he whisked it into a paper bag before picking up the money, poking a few keys on the cash register.

"Did you see?" I asked Dilly. "What'd she buy?"

"Will you shut up?" she said. "Just shut up, Rafe." She let go of my hand, stalked back to the soda counter.

I followed, watched Marilyn drop her change into her purse without counting it, walk back outside and into a convertible crookedly parked out front.

And just quick enough so you weren't sure she actually was there, she was gone.

Dilly was up on her stool, folding the soda straws into triangles. Her back was stiff like a cat halfway to a tussle. I sat next to her.

"What'd she buy?" I asked.

She shrugged. "Who cares?"

"Who cares! Nothing like this has ever happened before," I said. "Marilyn Monroe coming into Jack Dorry's drugstore and you ask who cares?" I put my hand in the crook of her elbow. Her skin was sticky with sweat, but soft, and I realized I'd never touched her exactly there before.

She brushed me away. "Leave me alone," she said.

"What's with you?" I asked.

The fat girl said, "I'm going to write up a report on you right this minute if you don't leave this girl alone." Her face was red, too, and she looked tired, like maybe her feet hurt all of a sudden. She poured Dilly a fresh glass of water without her asking.

"Thank you," Dilly said.

The girl nodded, said, "You're welcome."

Something was going on between them.

"You know what she bought," I said to Dilly. "Tell me."

Dilly turned to look straight at me. It was like she'd found herself a new face, like she'd never climbed a tree to the top or struck me out with bases loaded or wrestled me headfirst into a mud puddle or raced to the bottom of a soda or laughed a long trail of Os all ringed together. "She bought sanitary napkins," she said. Her voice stayed flat. "If you must know."

The fat girl glared at me.

Jack was in back where everyone knew he went to nip from his bottle.

It's not like I even knew exactly what they were, sanitary napkins. Only that I shouldn't ask anything else about them, about her.

A long minute later, Dilly said, "I'm sorry, Rafe. Let's get another soda. Want to?"

But it was late. I had to be getting home.

Marilyn Poses on Red Satin

Lyn Lifshin

She's heard it
will make her
tits more red,
leans back
tries to imagine
this, isn't
happy, like some-
one under someone
they'd never chose
who is pumping
away. She hears
a train whistle,
quietly hums a
few leaving blues,
has to pee but
doesn't. The
slick cloth is
cold as a strange
tongue wedged
deep inside her.
Blue would have
been more her
but red, the
photographer
whistled would
touch men's
blood make them
want to charge.

Marilyn Monroe Knows She Should Make Herself

Lyn Lifshin

get out from the
quilts blurring
the outside world
as much as valium
or phenobarb, a
cocoon she can
escape in, softness
to hold her, blur
edges, camouflage
what jabbed from
inside and out.
She doesn't want
to call the limo
for the studio,
work out, have her
hair yanked and
bleached. Today
she doesn't care
if this is the last
time they let her
thru the gate.
She hugs her pillow.
In another life she
might hot foot it

to take tap, pluck
her eyebrows shave
way up high as if
to clear a path
for heavy traffic
up inside her. In
another life she'd
stay Norma Jean,
just go to movies
not be in them, have
some Billy Jo who
wouldn't shoot her
on red satin with
not just her lips
parted, or shoot
air up under her
dress first check-
ing out her see thru
panties, but just
fill her soft and
slowly as feathers.

Marilyn Monroe Longs for a Siamese Twin

Lyn Lifshin

Nothing else
holds her as
close or long
enough. She
wants a double,
another who would
never care if she
lost muscle tone,
let her blond
go natural,
go gray. Roses
smell like
funerals she
whispers to the
mirror, lovers
die. Or go. I
want someone so
like me they
understand me,
not any old
siamese twin
but one who's
identical a
mirror me who

will know her
breasts and
legs are just
boobs and gams,
nothing unusual,
there to cushion
and be soft,
fill out an
angora sweater
soft as a cat,
someone to take
her out on the
town—they'd
be on their own
but never alone.

FROM The Missing Person

Doris Grumbach

It was Thursday, almost the end of a long week of shooting. Franny had worked four days without interruption. Thursday evening Reuben told her: "The rushes look good, Franny. Want to see them?"

She said no, and went home late and was sick on Friday. Arnie was in New York seeing his agent or someone, she wasn't sure who, so she was alone in the house except for Olivia at the other end. She lay on the couch thinking she'd be alone unless she called someone and said she was lonely and alone and would they come over. Through her head ran the old words and the scene: *Red rover red rover the little boys used to say and then tear across the road and knock me down and my vaccination scab bled all over my leg let Roger come over, they'd all shout.*

But she called no one. *It was Saturday when everybody makes plans*, she thought, *to be with their families or girlfriends, or someone.* Saturday was always a long day for her when she wasn't on location or working at the lot. The night, when Arnie was away, was always worse. She walked through the endless house until she found Olivia and told her she could go see her husband who got off at four from the hotel where he worked. Olivia said: "What about your dinner?"

Franny said she didn't need her, she'd make out fine, she'd find something in the refrigerator. Olivia didn't seem to want to go.

"You be all right by yourself, honey?"

"Oh, sure."

"What you do here by yourself?"

"Take a nap, Olivia. Don't worry."

Olivia shook her head. But as it approached three-thirty she packed up a supper for her husband and herself, and left. Franny took a pill and lay down on the couch. Nothing happened. She thought maybe another pill would do it. She wanted to sleep through tonight, through Sunday, through that night. After she took it she thought she heard the bell ring. It rang again. Lou, she thought, or maybe even Reuben, who sometimes came by after she'd been sick a day. Or Janet Faith, who had lived next door to Franny when she first came to Hollywood. *It might even be that bastard Brock*, she thought grimly, *who sometimes feels sorry for his behavior on the set and says so at the end of a hard week, or maybe Dolores who worries about me a lot.*

She went to the door, unbolted and unlocked it, and opened it to a short woman all in black except for a white fringe around her face, a cross hanging on her chest, and steel-rimmed glasses so thick Franny couldn't make out her eyes through them. *A nun, for God's sake. Is she following me from the school?*

"Are you sure you have the right place?" she asked.

"Yes, miss. I'm Sister Inez, a Parish Visitor. I'm taking the Catholic census of this neighborhood. Are you a Catholic?"

"God, no," Franny said. "Why?"

The Sister wrote something down on a paper she had stuck on a clipboard, and started to walk away. Franny (later she never knew why) suddenly said: "Will you, uh, would you like to come in?"

The Sister stopped, turned around, looked at Franny through glasses like the ends of binoculars, and hesitated. Then she said: "All right. If you want me to."

Franny led her into the parlor.

The Sister's black, floor-length clothing looked odd against all the white in the parlor. She took off a large, black shawl and folded it carefully over her arm.

Franny said: "Please sit down."

She did, on one of the hard white chairs under the window. She perched on the edge of it and watched warily as Franny stretched out on the couch. The silence grew heavy.

Then the Parish Visitor said: "Is there something I can do for you, miss?"

Franny couldn't think of anything to say, but she wanted to say something so that the Parish Visitor would stay, sitting there on the edge of the chair in the white parlor, like a blackbird in snow.

"Are you the one from the school downtown?" she asked politely, like a little girl making conversation to a grown-up.

The Sister looked confused. "No. I don't think so. But the Motherhouse for Parish Visitors is not too far from here."

Franny began to feel the effect of the two Seconals. She said apologetically to the Sister: "I'm a little tired. I hate to go to sleep when I'm alone."

The Sister nodded, as though to indicate that she understood this phenomenon. "Do you want me to stay with you until you fall asleep, miss?"

"Oh yes, I do. Thank you very much." Franny went to the bar at the far end of the room and poured herself a glass of grape juice with gin in it. She took another Seconal from a bottle she kept under the lip of the white bartop, and then stretched out again on the couch. She closed her eyes, waiting for the dark-red film to come over her eyes, *like grape juice, like blood, after I have enough gin and pills, the slow coming on of sleep, not black, not yet, only red and then purple. . . .*

But the black did not come. Franny opened her eyes. The Parish Visitor was sitting there, still bolt upright, her eyes closed, a string of black beads in her hands. She seemed to be talking to herself.

Franny's voice trembled. "What are you *saying*?"

"I'm praying."

"For *me*?" Franny asked in a shocked voice.

"What?"

"Are you saying prayers for me?"

"For the whole world, miss. *In saeculi saeculorum.* For us all. For you too."

Franny shut her eyes. Sleep was just beyond her, across a blood-red chasm she could see with her eyes closed. She thought: *one more pill and some grape-juice gin will do the trick, take me across.* One more pill and it wouldn't matter that Arnie was in New York talking to people who would know how to answer him. She remembered that when that happened his eyes didn't look empty, the way they looked behind his glasses when he looked at her, seeing nothing in her, judging her the way her mother used to do when she looked at her.

Franny went to the bar, and then lay down on the couch. She woke to find the Parish Visitor standing over her, holding her wrist. Franny saw she was wearing a thick plain silver wedding ring. A *nun?* she wondered and then she felt herself falling asleep again. Dark-red blood filled the pits around her eyeballs, and leaked out of the holes of her ears. . . .

The Sister was shaking Franny, pushing at her face, slapping her. Franny muttered in her sleep: "What's a Parish Visitor?" And the Sister said, "Your eyes look strange, miss."

Franny said, "I'm fine. I need to sleep." The Sister pinched Franny's cheeks gently, trying to keep her awake.

"The wedding ring," said Franny flatly, although she had meant to ask a question. She lay still, her eyes shut.

The Sister said: "Bride of Christ, miss. Please sit up and stay awake. Have you taken something?"

"Not a thing," mumbled Franny. "Tired."

"At six o'clock in the evening? You look strange."

"Say the prayers. I'll just sleep a little."

The Parish Visitor turned the beads around in her hand, praying in a low voice.

"Pay for us now and Indy whirl to comb," Franny thought the Parish Visitor said. She felt herself being covered with something, and before she could ask what the words meant she was asleep.

For the rest of the evening, the Parish Visitor sat on the edge of the couch, letting Franny sleep a little and then slapping her awake. She said the rosary twice and then read from a small black book she had taken from her pocket.

At ten, she stood up, putting the rosary and the prayer book into her pocket and throwing the shawl around her shoulders. She said: "I must go, miss. They'll worry about me at the convent where I stay."

Franny heard her, dimly, but could not summon up enough energy to respond, and then fell back into a deep, dreamless sleep.

At midnight she woke to find Olivia there, her brown face having faded into place over the Parish Visitor's white-bread face. Franny said nothing to her about the nun, never told anyone (except Mary Maguire much later) about her coming that night, and was not sure, sometimes, that she had been there at all. But she believed that the Sister, sitting there and praying for her and for all the world with those blind eyes and black beads and the silver Bride-of-Christ wedding ring, had pulled her from the red-running stream of death and nothing-ness into some saving place. She thought her rescue may have depended on the incantation the Parish Visitor kept saying. She was always to remember her as a person who had words, like Arnie, and she believed that the magic of the words had saved her. Her regret was that the Parish Visitor had gone off to the Motherhouse without telling her what they were, what they meant. She had lost her chance for salvation.

Marilyns

(a f t e r W a r h o l)

Jeanne Beaumont

Marilyn
    as a battered child
        as a woman who got her
makeup on wrong
           Marilyn as demon
with her eyes open
             with her eyes closing, closed
      Marilyn as goddess, riddle
Marilyn having a bad day
      Marilyn in shadow
          up from the coal mines,
             punched, bruised
Marilyn as
      plain, garish, girlish, gritting her teeth
smiling, licking her lips, starting to speak—
               muted
As rich girl, spoiled rotten, poor thing, cheap
    (Marilyn as ghost, ghoulish) ghastly
defaced, partly erased, only surface
      Marilyn revealed, vanishing . . .
blackened, blotted, blurred, blemished
    Marilyn in a wig
      with running mascara
        with stained teeth
        (post-berry-eating)
on-screen Marilyn, behind screen, through—
    blown up, lined up, covered up, flat
    rose lips, sealed lips, parted lips, (parts)

Marilyn as bearded woman, beauty
                        black and white or
            cutie—orange aqua red
                                    Come-on Marilyn
Instructions for use:
            mask, mother, everywoman, nun—
Choose one. This is a factory run.

There's fifty more where these came from.

FROM Queen of Desire

Sam Toperoff

LIGHTS

LIFE: In so many interviews you've given, you allude frequently to your childhood in a way that makes one think of an unwanted waif. Could it really have been as bad as all that?

MONROE: It wasn't pleasant. Sure, there were times when individuals treated me well, but they were few and far between. A child knows when she's unwanted—my God, how could I miss it? One month I was hustled off to this so-called "relative," the next month in a foster home, and then back with my mother whenever they let her out of the mental hospital. I won't even mention the Los Angeles Orphans' Home. It wasn't pretty. You see kids who are loved, who have stability and normal human affection, so you know exactly what you are being denied.

LIFE: Heavens, that conjures visions of Dickens, *Oliver Twist*, beatings with a cane, bowls of gruel, dirty-faced street urchins. Surely it couldn't have been that bad.

MONROE: I don't really want to get into specifics. What's to be gained? It sounds like you're complaining or looking for sympathy. Almost like a "Tell me how hard your life was" deal. It's too depressing.

LIFE: But it would help people understand what makes an individual tick, especially when the individual is talented and widely admired. Isn't it possible, for example, that the events that marked your childhood, unpleasant though they may be to contemplate, actually had the effect of shaping you into the creative personality that has emerged?

MONROE: Funny you say that, because it's the question that's on my mind all the time these days. Sometimes I believe in my heart I would have become what I did even if I had an "apple pie" childhood. Then there are times when I'm one hundred percent certain I became an actress and have driven myself to be better precisely because of the childhood I had. I know it forced me deeper into myself, made me develop an imagination—I know it drove me to want to prove to the world I was somebody, that it couldn't beat me down.

LIFE: Well, which one was it?

MONROE: Probably both . . . and neither. Or is that too Zen?

C A M E R A

Marilyn was at the Alcott and Murchison Funeral Home in Santa Monica. She wore a tailored suit, black linen, a black straw hat with a wide tilted brim, pulled taut by a tulle veil that tied under her chin. She had flown in from New York, where she was studying with Lee Strasberg at The Actors Studio, preparing, as the columnists were all speculating, for her stage debut.

In the open casket, "Aunt" Ana Lower, the aunt of her mother's best friend. "Aunt" Ana was indeed a great woman. Norma Jean lived with her in a large rambling house in Santa Monica for thirteen months when she was ten. Ana Lower offered the girl the purest, most nourishing love Norma Jean would ever have in her life. Now Marilyn gazed at the wonderful woman, whose tiny, shriveled body offered fraudulent evidence of what once had been.

Relatives and friends were, for the most part, keeping their distance. The wife of a cousin sat down alongside Mar-

ilyn and asked for an autograph for her children. Marilyn looked for help while she signed. Mr. Murchison came to her aid and led Marilyn up to the casket.

Ana's eyes were closed. Marilyn recalled eyes as gray and clear as a pencil sketch. The face was spotted and deeply lined; it used to have a soft pink glow Marilyn took for a standard of good health. This was not the person who saved Marilyn's sanity; this was the dry husk of what was left when that person had given out.

Norma Jean was brought to live with the sixty-two-year-old spinster lady after her tenth birthday. The child did not consciously decide to stop talking, as her mother, Gladys Baker, believed. Gladys was certain her child was being purposely difficult. It was as though one day she was a bright and active little chirper; the next, a sick, silent bird.

The man with the mustache had been one of her mother's friends. They had gone on nice picnics with him, to the zoo, even on a trip to Santa Monica to visit Ana Lower.

As Marilyn tried to look into the woman in the coffin, she considered touching the back of the dead hand. Had she thanked her enough for saving her soul? The man's name came to her just then. For the first time in more than twenty years. Harley Lowes.

It was 1935. Gladys was home again, working at the studio after a brief hospitalization for a nervous breakdown. Marilyn saw the room clearly too—the wallpaper in aqua tints, the stuccoed ceiling, billowing white curtains, Grand Rapids maple furniture, and mirrors: a mirror running the length of the closet door, another on the face of the armoire, and a three-way makeup mirror on the dressing table. Her mother loved mirrors; once, when Norma Jean asked why, she said, "Mirrors make more light. Let there be light," and then something in French.

Marilyn remembered another strange thing in the room: a single silver candlestick on top of the armoire. What had happened to it? Where was it now? Where was any of that stuff?

He was a young man, she realized now, in his mid-twenties perhaps, but she was so young all adults were old to her. Why, why in the world would her mother leave her alone *with him? She began to see it all again through childish eyes. Even in death, "Aunt" Ana had helped her to understand. Marilyn touched the dead hand.*

As she leaned near the body in the Alcott and Murchison Funeral Home, Marilyn whispered the first thing she'd ever said into "Aunt" Ana's sacks. "I don't ever want to be in the world without you, Gram." She had said it into the "Good Things" sack.

ACTION

Norma Jean keeps her gaze on his wispy mustache. It is very different from the photograph her mother showed her once, which she associated with the word "father." She knows this man isn't her father, but her mother likes him so much. Cleaned the apartment all morning, gave him two cups of coffee, even let him put his feet up on the fancy ottoman. Walked him through the sickroom, saying, "It's nothing, just a fever, a runny nose. I'm taking precautions. You think I'm too much of a doting mother?"

"No, not at all. It means you love her. Doesn't she, Norma?"

Norma Jean is selecting a crayon. If her mother likes him, she likes him too. She likes that he's never tried to play up to her or talk to her in a fake voice. But she keeps watching him, curiously, from her cluttered bed, where she is coloring pictures in *Ben, the Firehouse Dog.* She colors the fireman's red slicker aggressively, not bound by the outline. When she turns the pages, she peeks at the man till the moment she senses he's going to look at her. Then another mad scribble.

"Why don't I drive you?" the young man tells Gladys.

" 'Cause I don't want to leave her alone."

"But what could happen? Nothing."

"That's not the point. You just don't leave a sick nine-year-old alone. You just don't do it."

Norma sees how naturally he places his hands on her mother's shoulders and how she smiles back.

"So why," he says, "don't you let me drive to the studio and pick up the stuff? Just call so they'll expect me."

Gladys makes her sourpuss face. Norma knows nothing can change her mind. "No one but employees in the cutting room. Studio rule. It'll take twenty minutes. No more." Her voice softens and gets childish, a mannerism Norma Jean has noticed only when there's a man with her. "What's the matter, Mr. Lowes, a problem letting a woman drive your precious automobile?"

Mr. Lowes smooths his mustache with a thumb and forefinger.

Gladys's eyes bulge peculiarly. "Just as well. I'll call a cab."

"Don't be silly." Mr. Lowes digs in his pocket for the keys. "It pulls a little to the left when you brake. Just ease them, don't come down too hard."

Gladys is more than coy as she takes his car keys: "Tell me, when've I ever been too rough, Harley?"

Norma bites her lip, making it seem as if her choice of crayons puzzles her.

"Mommy's got to leave for a little while, honey. Mr. Lowes is going to stay with you till I come back." Gladys Baker hasn't ever referred to herself as "Mommy" in Norma's presence. The "honey" has never been used very much, and never so sweetly as this.

Since her mother believes she's ill, Norma obliges and manufactures a thin cough.

"I'll pick up some cough drops while I'm out. And how about some vanilla ice cream? It's good for your throat."

Norma doesn't respond. She puts her red crayon back in the place reserved for it in the tin. It's time to start on Ben himself, the firehouse dog. He's sitting in the seat next to the driver of the engine. Like Ben, Norma has her tongue pointed intently out of her mouth.

"I said, should I pick up some ice cream?"

Norma heard the offer the first time. She hates vanilla. That's the flavor her mother likes.

"Sure," Mr. Lowes says, "get some ice cream. Here." He takes a roll of bills out of his pocket and pulls off a dollar, and another.

"I've got money. It's Norma Jean. She hasn't said she wants ice cream. Have you?"

23

Norma bites her tongue and begins to color Ben. Because she has never seen a Dalmatian, she reverses the coloring. The black spots she leaves white, the white background she strokes in black, deep gray actually. "Uh-uh."

"Is that a yes or a no?"

"Don't like vanilla."

"That's what's good for a cold, vanilla. That's what they give you in the hospital, vanilla."

Mr. Lowes says, "The flavor don't matter. Just that it's cold. It soothes the throat. Here." He flutters the bills. "Get her what she wants. You and me, we'll have vanilla."

"So what kind?"

Norma Jean does not look up from her work. "Something with fruit."

"Other kids, it's vanilla or chocolate. My kid, it's something with fruit." Almost casually, she takes the money.

"And why don't you get us a pack of Camels too," he says.

Gladys Baker goes into her bedroom to select shoes and a hat. Mr. Lowes wanders around Norma's bedroom, first peering out the window at his Studebaker, then shaking her piggy bank—to which he adds a quarter—and reordering her blocks alphabetically. He leans over Norma to inspect her coloring. He says unconvincingly, "That's very good."

Norma smells him. He is wet wool and caramel. He smells her. She is warm grass and cough medicine.

Mr. Lowes wanders out of the bedroom. Norma hears his voice coming from her mother's room. She darkens Ben's coat to a deeper gray, aware of their distant voices. She cannot discern words; the tone, however, is new. Her mother's laugh is unusually rough. Mr. Lowes speaks softly and slurringly, like a radio that isn't tuned in properly. Norma is still, holding her breath, listening.

Then her mother, completely dressed, buttoning her pale yellow Easter coat, comes into the bedroom. Mr. Lowes stands in the doorway and smiles like a friend at Norma, as her mother places a hand on her daughter's forehead and scowls.

"Fever?" Mr. Lowes asks.

"A little warm."

"Got a thermometer?"

"Norma Jean hates it."

"Which kind?" He places his finger in his mouth and then behind his rump.

"That kind," Gladys says. "Okay now, young lady." The "young lady," too, is only for guests. "If you need anything, just call Mr. Lowes. Some juice. You're supposed to drink lots of juice. Where's your handkerchief?"

Norma pulls an unused, neatly folded handkerchief from the sleeve of her flowered nightie.

"Okay. Don't be ashamed to go to the bathroom."

Embarrassed, Norma Jean looks to the visitor for help. He indicates a secret alliance with pursed lips and a faint nod. She immediately turns to her coloring book and reaches for a yellow crayon to color number 74 on the fire engine.

Gladys kisses Norma Jean's forehead. "I'll be right back with the ice cream. And don't be such a sourpuss."

"We'll be fine, Gladys," he says.

Her mother moves past Mr. Lowes, and he runs his hand across her back and follows her out to the living room. Norma hears the front door close. Then a snap that might be the lock. After a minute or so, music comes from the big cabinet radio in the living room, Russ Columbo singing "Prisoner of Love."

He steps into her doorway. "You like that music?"

She strings out her answer, trying for the same coyness she's heard from Gladys: "Yeah."

Stroking his mustache, he comes alongside her bed. "You don't really have a fever, do you?"

"I might," still coy with her eyes and her tongue. "I usually wear a bow in my hair. The yellow one."

"You want your bow now?"

"Yeah."

Lowes brings the ribbon to her.

"I don't know how to tie it." Even while speaking, Norma turns in her bed, putting her back to Lowes. "She puts it under my hair and ties it up like on a package." Norma lifts her soft brown hair and bends her neck forward. It is long and slender and very white. He is reminded of a swan. He sits down on the edge of her bed and places the ribbon flat against that neck. She drops her hair over it.

At just the moment he is pulling the second loop through the ribbon, Norma Jean looks back at him in a curious way. Her hair smells like perfumed soap. There seems to be a warmth coming off her vulnerable little body. He feels as though he is doing something terribly wrong. He ties a large, irregular bow high in her hair.

He realizes he is in an inviolate place; it frightens him. It excites him.

Norma Jean asks, "Do you have a sister?"

"Why?"

"Just want to know."

"Why?"

"I just thought . . ." The rest of the thought is dismissed with a fetching shrug.

Harley Lowes knows he is aroused, has been since he saw and then touched her delicate neck. He won't actually do anything wrong, but it's too soon to leave her bed. He tells himself he won't let things go too far.

"So what do you like to do when you're not drawing?"

"I'm not drawing. I'm coloring."

"Oh, coloring. Yeah."

"You're not supposed to say 'yeah.' You're supposed to say 'yes.' "

Like a child himself, he says, "I heard you say 'yeah.' "

"You like my mom?"

"Sure. Why?"

"No reason." For the first time, Norma looks directly into his eyes and lets the glance linger. Lowes becomes conscious of the fact that the child is extremely beautiful. He catches his breath. There is still room to maneuver; he has not gone too far. He knows he ought to leave.

"Let me see your fingers." He very much wants to touch her hand: that's all, touch her hand. She puts down the crayon and offers her hand to him palm up. He treats it as something rare. It feels warm and begins to quiver as he squeezes it slightly. She starts to pull it away. He looks into her face; her tongue is folded over her lower lip. His breath catches in his chest. He squeezes her hand tight. He has an erection pushing down the leg he has angled on the bed by Norma's side. Their eyes meet again and he looks down, trying to draw her gaze to the swelling on his thigh. His temples throb with his heartbeat.

Norma Jean's voice is a whisper. "I know what that is."

"No you don't."

"I do."

"How?"

"I won't tell."

He doesn't want it to be his voice, so he removes himself from the words. "You can touch it."

"No."

"There's nothing wrong." He brings her hand to his leg and brushes her fingertips along his swollen penis. Norma has no expression on her face. She feels only the texture of the wool. Excitement pushes him to the edge of control. He closes his eyes and breathes through his mouth in rhythm to the stroking.

She tries to withdraw her hand. The breathing, though, and the baring of his lower teeth have frightened her. The pupils of his eyes appear to have darkened, appear tinged with red. She tugs her hand suddenly, and he lets go.

"You shouldn't do that. You're not allowed."

He's reluctant to look at her face. "Why not?"

There's no answer. He hears the rippling of crayon on paper again. The radio is playing "Sunny Side of the Street." When he stands, the swelling in his crotch hardens again. Norma Jean says, "What are you doing?"

He intended to leave the bedroom, but he says, "I'm looking for the thermometer. I told your mom I'd take care of you."

"I don't want that."

"Where's the thermometer?"

"I don't like it."

On a shelf in the bathroom, the thermometer is next to a small jar of Vaseline. "Nothing to worry about. You're probably normal."

"You're not supposed to do it."

He comes back into the bedroom, shaking down the thermometer. They look at each other. Lowes says, "Let's surprise your mother. We'll prove to her you don't have a temperature."

"I don't."

"We have to be sure. We don't want to lie. You'll have to take off your panties."

"I don't have any on."

"Fine. Then pull back the cover."

Norma Jean shakes her head. Lowes pulls the patchwork quilt easily out of her hands down to her ankles. *Ben, the Firehouse Dog* and a handful of crayons fall off the bed. Slowly, she pulls her knees to her chest; it is a protective reflex, which Lowes perceives as inviting because the child's calves and the back of her thighs are revealed as the hem of her nightgown is lifted. Her face is quizzical. She looks exactly like her mother.

Lowes begins to speak and abruptly catches himself. He unscrews the Vaseline and rolls the tip of the thermometer in the lubricant. Norma Jean doesn't move. He rescrews the cap and sits down on the bed.

Norma says, "Don't look."

Lowes turns his head away slightly and guides the thermometer into the darkness beneath her nightgown. He can feel it brush the inside of her thigh. When it touches her vagina, Norma Jean tenses. He does not stop. He probes the area delicately. The thermometer enters the tight fold. "Not there," Norma says.

Still he probes. He feels it continue into the girl. She squirms slightly and says, "Not there."

He waggles his wrist and it enters deeper still. For the first time, there's insistence in her voice. "No. Don't."

He stops, but doesn't withdraw the thermometer. "I have a sister. I did this with her. When she was sick in bed. It was okay to do."

"It isn't. Stop or I'll tell."

"You won't. You better not."

"I will."

Lowes withdraws the thermometer slowly. His expression perplexes Norma Jean: he looks like the one who's been insulted. He picks up the Vaseline jar and goes into the bathroom. She hears the water running, the medicine chest open and close. He emerges, patting his face with wet hands.

Pulling her cover over herself again, Norma begins to frown. He takes it for the onset of tears. "Don't cry. Your temperature is normal."

"You didn't take it. I know what you did." But her frown is caused by the book and the crayons out of reach on the floor. Lowes bends and picks them up, putting them gently next to the girl.

"Remember, I'm the one who got you the kind of ice cream you wanted."

Norma seeks the page she has been working on. "It's only ice cream."

"*Only* ice cream. That's a fine thing to say. You ever hear the saying 'Looking a gift horse in the mouth'?"

"Nope." She's coloring the fire engine again.

"You're supposed to stay inside the lines."

"If you want to." Her manner is coy again. Her tongue comes out.

Lowes takes a thin black comb from his rear pocket and runs it straight back through his light hair, which falls neatly in waves on his head. Norma watches, impressed. So he does it again. "You have nice hair too," he says.

"My mother says it's mousy."

"It's not. She's wrong."

"It used to be real light. It's turning. I'm gonna tell Mama what you did."

Lowes leaves a long silence. Norma colors and hums so softly and intermittently it might not be humming but the breeze or another, more distant, radio.

"I was worried about your cold. I took your temperature."

"Oh, sure."

Her tone scares Harley Lowes. He walks out of her bedroom and peers from the front window for his car coming down the street. Before he sees it, he unlocks the door and walks out on the front steps. He lights a cigarette. He is ashamed and frightened.

His car turns into Grove Street. Gladys is driving too fast and too far in the center of the road. Lowes looks for cars coming from the other direction; there are none. She turns too sharply into the driveway and hits the edge of the curb jarringly. Lowes scowls and forces a smile when Gladys waves.

He approaches and helps her out. She has a pile of folders and a film canister. "The ice cream?" he reminds. She picks two hand-packed containers off the floor.

"How'd it go?" she wants to know.

"With Norma Jean? Fine. We took her temperature." Gladys Baker looks a little surprised. She says, "Oh."

"She was normal."

They all have their ice cream, Norma Jean in her bed. Lowes and Gladys talk for a while out in the living room. Then Lowes leaves, earlier than planned. He doesn't say goodbye to Norma Jean; she hears him tell her mother, "I think she's sleeping. She needs her sleep."

Norma Jean didn't tell her mother anything the next day, or even the following week. The two spoke so little, Gladys didn't realize for months that Norma had developed a worrisome stutter. Finally, a note came home from school saying that Norma Jean was acting strangely and could she please make an appointment to come to school. She didn't respond, and the school contacted her again.

Norma Jean refused to speak when she was asked a direct question by her teacher. There were rare occasions when she spoke, softly and briefly, but most of the time she just shook her head. Eventually, she didn't speak at all. She did everything the teachers asked. She did all her homework. But the teachers were concerned because Norma Jean had been such a normal, outgoing girl. This was all very strange; they were worried. What had happened? Gladys certainly didn't know.

The girl wasn't exactly choosing not to speak; either something was blocking the process from thought to word or it was broken. She had thoughts, she had a few things she wanted to say; there was simply no reason to say them, no impulse to propel them, no desire to share them.

Hardly anyone in those days understood psychological

trauma, although the school principal mentioned the word "psychiatrist." The word, the suggestion, offended Gladys Baker. Her daughter would not be crazy. The problem did not keep Gladys from seeing Harley Lowes. He came to the house for dinner one night and brought Norma Jean a box of chocolates. Norma took it into her room. Rarely after that did he come to the house; he picked Gladys up at the studio. Those nights, Norma made her own supper.

At school, the assumption was that her stutter was the reason she didn't speak. She was assigned a speech teacher for an hour each day. Norma spoke haltingly with the teacher for a while and then stopped speaking entirely. The teacher advised that nothing be done: when the child wanted to speak again, she would. This was a reasonable assumption, which Gladys did not have the patience to allow to run its course. She would go a few days without badgering the child and then suddenly explode at dinner, insisting that Norma Jean drop the damn act and start talking.

Those nights Norma Jean cried herself to sleep. Gladys believed the weeping was better than the silence, a step on the way to speaking again. Speech didn't come while Norma Jean lived with her mother.

One night, Gladys did not come home from the studio. Norma opened a can of tuna fish and toasted bread for a sandwich. At the kitchen table, she drew a map of Africa for her geography homework. The telephone rang after she was in bed. It wasn't her mother; it was Grace McKee, her mother's best friend at work.

Gladys had been hospitalized again. Norma stayed a short while with Grace McKee and her husband. Then she stayed with Grace's aunt, Ana Lower.

When Norma Jean arrived at "Aunt" Ana's house in Santa Monica, it was one of the largest farmhouses in town. Its east façade still looked out over sloping farmland with a view that stretched to distant mountains. Times were very hard; Ana had turned the place into a rooming house. There were five or six families sharing the premises, but most of the men were looking for work far away and were never there for more than a day or two. It was a house of women and children. Meals were shared; so were the tasks and chores.

Norma was happy there, especially when she came home from school and the large kitchen was quiet for about an hour while Ana baked a pie or prepared muffins for dinner. Norma loved to help the woman she called "Gram." She had been there for three months and had become a happier child, but changing schools twice had been difficult. She had stopped speaking again.

Norma keeps the screen door from slamming and tiptoes across the linoleum. All the familiar baking paraphernalia is on the table. Ana, in a pinafore apron, has her back to the door.

Ana knows her sweet girl is approaching and holds in a laugh while letting the child near. She begins to hum while wiping an already dry plate with a dish towel.

Ana hears Norma's soft breath and then feels cool hands on her cheeks just below her eyes. "Oh, my, who's that? It can't be . . . ?" She spins. "Oh my, it is. It's the Princess Casamassima." Ana curtsies. Norma dips even lower. They hug.

"I've got a tiny piece of pie left. And some chocolate milk. The Princess would like?"

Norma nods.

Ana takes a cold plate with a slice of peach pie and a bottle of milk from the huge gas refrigerator. Norma sits at the kitchen table. Ana fetches a tall glass and a tin of chocolate syrup. The sounds of pouring, the clinking of the spoon against the thick glass, are especially distinct.

"I've been doing some thinking, Princess. It isn't good for you not to talk. Not good because you have to hold too much inside yourself. You might explode."

There's a frown on Norma's brow.

"See what I've got." From below the table, the old lady elevates two paper sacks. She has printed in bold blue crayon letters the words "Good Things" on one sack and "Bad Things" on the other.

Norma's frown gives way to interest.

"Here's what I figured. Of course, it may be a very foolish thing. You don't have to talk to me, not to anyone. But if you have something to get off your chest, something that's bothering you or something you're really happy about, why not just whisper it in the sack. I'll have them here every day when you come home. Your secret sacks. Anything in your heart you can whisper in them."

So simple, so profound an idea. Ana Lower understood the mysteries of the human heart; she was the saving psychologist in a time and place where there was no one else.

The very next afternoon, Norma comes into the kitchen with a secret smile on her lips. The sacks are on the table. Ana, at the sink, turns and folds her arms. Norma puts her books on a kitchen chair. Their eyes lock. Norma kneels on the chair next to her books and leans her chin into the "Good Things" sack.

The whispered sounds come to Ana's ears like lovely music.

Every day for a month, Norma spoke into her sacks. Ana also brought them up to Norma's bedroom every night before bed. Soon after, the girl whispered to her directly. A while after that, she spoke softly at dinner to some of Ana's boarders. It took longer for her to speak at school, but eventually she volunteered to spell the word "friendly" in class. Then it was over: Norma Jean spoke quietly but as normally as any of the girls in her class.

Norma Jean would have stayed with Ana for years, but Ana's health had begun to fail; she was living in constant pain.

Marilyn Monroe never forgot the majesty of "Aunt" Ana. Or her debt to her. The two paper sacks were the end of insult and humiliation, of shame and guilt. Ana was also the midwife of her imagination, of confidence, of the breathless Marilyn whisper.

Saturday Afternoon, June, Long Island, New York

Julia P. Dubner

Marilyn lies by the pool, trying to finish *Ulysses* with the kids crawling all over her. Their hair is dripping with chlorine water and they smell like bars of soap. She is trying to finish and they won't leave her alone.

Arthur told her in the car that today was not the day. "Just eat a frankfurter and be beautiful," he said. "Since when are you so literate anyway?"

Marilyn wanted to smack him but he was driving. Every night she's been reading until three A.M., and he doesn't even notice her side of the bed's empty. She's determined. Today *is* the day.

Marilyn's trying to finish and the neighbors are looking through the fence, peeking through the knotholes like she's a rare bug. Do they notice her legs aren't shaved?

"Get a tan," Arthur said, "it'll make you look healthy."

Look healthy? As if the illusion is all she can hope for. She reads too much into his every word, but he must know what he's doing with them. Words are his business, right? She reads *Ulysses* for herself, but also for him. Arthur won't see that, though, won't see how she's telling him she can live in his world, too.

Arthur's brother finishes the burgers and the kids scamper away from her, finally. The tall teenage boys, gangly and aggressive, push their way ahead of the smaller cousins. Marilyn's not interested in burgers, can't be interested in burgers. The sun is low now, skimming off the harsh blue pool water. She has to wear sunglasses for the glare. It's not a movie star thing, despite what the neighbors probably think.

Alexa, Arthur's niece, pokes a burger in Marilyn's face. "Don'tcha want some, Aunt Marilyn? They're really good." A teardrop of ketchup sits at the corner of Alexa's mouth, stretching and getting small again with every word.

"No, honey, but thanks. And don't call me aunt. Aunts are old and pickled."

"I've got pickles, too." Alexa opens the bun, revealing a gob of mayonnaise with two kosher dill eyes.

It's no use, they're all back at the pool now, big ones, small ones, surrounding her chaise, talking with their mouths full.

The playground is the closest escape: the merry-go-round. None of their mothers will let them near the merry-go-round for at least another hour—they'd all vomit burgers and carrot sticks and smell up the Buicks on the way home.

Marilyn wishes for a wooden horse or frog to spirit her away, but there's only the metal circle of narrow, peeling-orange-paint benches. She can handle it, though. Anything to get away, to finish. Just twenty-five more pages, Molly Bloom thinking without a breath; it's torture to have to keep closing the book.

Arthur glances up from the picnic table as she walks away from the pool—just a quick look. He's pretending not to be interested in her these days. His little game.

Picnics were never right, never the right place to have fun. Food and outside don't go together, Marilyn's mother once told her, and it's true. Food is for inside, when you're not feeling like part of the rest of the world. Picnics try to be natural but what are you doing? Wrapping everything in wax paper and worrying about ants.

Reading outside is different. Arthur always reads in his big leather chair, a tumbler of scotch rocks click-clacking beside him, the bulb inches from his head. He reads with one hand, shakes the tumbler with the other. Marilyn needs the air, needs to hear the pages flap, feel some wind on her neck. Otherwise it's painful, reading. Lightbulbs hurt her eyes. Too still, when you're sitting and nothing around you moves and just the walls are breathing, watching.

The children are probably scared of her now. Too deliberate, walking away like that. Arthur says she's moody and he's right. But she hates all these kids today: they know she's afraid of the water, but they splashed her and dripped and pulled on her ankles. Alexa's hands—cold and pruny, a cat's tongue, an old woman's hands—grabbed around her ankles.

Alexa's the one Arthur loves, says she's got a brain as well as a belly on her. He said this on the way here, while rubbing Marilyn's stomach.

"And I don't have a brain?" But Arthur didn't answer. He doesn't like to talk real talk when he's driving. Says he gets too involved, loses the road under him.

The merry-go-round starts turning as Marilyn sits. She brakes with her toe in the dirt, then brings her knees up for a little table. The sun is just right, at her back, no glare—as if she's been arranging this all along, with some inside line to God and the weather-makers. She could take the sunglasses off, but she'll keep them on for the curious neighbors.

"Family is what you've always wanted," Arthur said in the car, "so why are you fussing? Family, dogs, the whole nine yards today."

"A family of my own. Not *your* family."

"You hate your family."

"No."

"All of them who are still alive." He rubbed her thigh. "Come on, sing with the radio for me."

Marilyn didn't. She knew he was mad by the way he held the steering wheel, switching from elbow out the window, easy thumb-hook to a perfect ten o'clock–two o'clock grip. Precision was Arthur's weapon.

Marilyn can be just as precise today, with her little knee-table and sunglasses and book. A perfect tea party for one, no boys allowed. Nothing to stop her from battling his silence with her own. She's got Molly Bloom. Molly and her flowers and no one telling her what to think.

But Marilyn doesn't think like Molly Bloom. You need a big piece of quiet to think like that, all in one sentence. Quiet inside and out, even with a lover and a husband.

Screams come from the pool, and Alexa is running around the shallow end, faster than her boy cousins. They're trying to untie her top and she's howling for them to go away, holding the string around her neck with one hand, the string around her back with the other, waddling, elbows out, still faster than the bloated boys.

Don't come by me, I can't save you, Marilyn thinks, gripping her toes to the metal bench, hoping to keep still and invisible. Fend for yourself, little girl, because you can and you'll always have to.

Arthur's brother unceremoniously shoos the boys away, then tells Alexa to keep away from them because she knows that's what they're going to do so why take her chances? Alexa sits in a ball in the shade of the water slide, rocking back and forth. She looks at Marilyn for the eyes behind the sunglasses.

Like a secret code, Marilyn takes off the glasses and hooks them to her shirt. Alexa accepts, comes out from under the slide and starts slowly toward the merry-go-round. The littlest boy cousin gets up to follow her, trying to prove himself to the others with stealth and bug eyes. He signals with a tinny "Hey" and in a second it's an all-out chase, the merry-go-round the finish line. Alexa gets there first, jumps on, starts it spinning.

Bracing her back against the metal, Marilyn holds on, dropping the book to her lap. The boys surround the merry-go-round, push faster so she has to close her eyes to keep her stomach down. Alexa screams, but Marilyn can't say anything, can't open her mouth. The book tumbles off her lap to the ground. The sky is gone, the sun, everything is gone.

Finally the spinning slows and Marilyn cracks an eyelid. Alexa is opposite her, their toes almost touching. The boys jump and run toward the pool, volleying *Ulysses* back and forth, playing Keep Away from the littlest. Still dizzy, Marilyn couldn't stand up even if she wanted to, but Alexa is there, silently asking her to stay.

Ulysses flies high above the boys' heads, dangerously close to the pool. Marilyn grabs Alexa's hand, more for her own protection than for the little girl's, and together they watch the pages flutter, hear the binding slap into the water. The boys separate, looking only slightly ashamed, and the book floats quietly, making its way toward the shallow end.

FROM Motor City

Bill Morris

The day the first-half sales figures hit his desk was a day Ted Mackey would never forget—not because the numbers looked so good but because it was the day he spoke with Marilyn Monroe for the first time.

"Hello? Mr. Mackey? Hello?" The voice coming through the transcontinental telephone static was surprisingly bird-like. He'd expected a husky voice, something from the bottom of a whisky barrel.

"Yes! This is Ted Mackey!"

"I can barely hear you. Can you hear me?"

"Yes, Miss . . . Mrs. . . . Shall I call you—"

"Call me Marilyn. That's my name." She laughed. Then there were several seconds of static. Ted had never in his life been struck dumb by a woman. Finally she said, "My manager tells me you have a very interesting proposition for me."

"Um . . . yes . . . Marilyn. We . . . I . . . What I wanted to talk to you about is actually a bit of a secret."

"Oooh, I *love* secrets."

"I'm afraid this one may not seem very juicy to you, but believe me, it's big news here in Detroit. Are you familiar by any chance with the Chevrolet Corvette?"

"You mean there's actually a car called a Carvette?"

"No, it's a *Corvette*. It's a two-seat sports car. Very sexy. A big seller, too. Here at the Buick Division we're coming out with a two-seat sports car of our own and—"

"You mean there isn't even a back seat?"

"No, just two front seats."

"What good is a car without a back seat?" Lusty laughter came through the static. Then Ted got it. He'd read in a tabloid that when Marilyn was married as a teenager, one of her favorite places to make love was the back seat of a car, preferably when it was parked on a city street. Once, when her husband protested that they might be discovered by a passerby, Marilyn supposedly cooed, "It's all right, honey, we're *married!*"

"I realize a car without a back seat is a little out of the ordinary," Ted said. "And to be honest with you, it's a bit of a gamble. Which is why I called you. I'd like for you to appear as the star of our advertising campaign for this new car—print, TV, radio, the works. We're calling the car the Wildcat, and I'd like you to be the Wildcat Girl."

"The Wildcat Girl. I like that, Ted. But I don't even have a driver's license."

"Somehow I think we can get around that."

"Well, I'll have to talk it over with my husband and my manager. We're in rehearsals right now for my new picture, so this isn't a good time."

"What's your new movie called?"

"*The Seven Year Itch.* We're supposed to do some location work in New York in the fall. Where are you located again?"

"I'm in Detroit."

"Is that near New York?"

"Not too far. I'm sure we could get together in New York if that would be convenient for you."

Someone—DiMaggio?—was yelling at her. "I've gotta run," she said. "Send us something and we'll talk again soon."

After that, the first-half sales figures were almost beside the point. Buick had sold 267,789 cars through June 30, exceeding even Ted Mackey's expectations and shattering all records.

It was a hot, sunny morning. Though summer was far from spent, the majestic elms around the Oakland Hills clubhouse were already beginning to shade to gold. On this weekday morning there were only a few women lying in lounge chairs by the swimming pool. Ted Mackey stripped off his seersucker shirt, stretched out, and let his thoughts drift from the upcoming Michigan football season, to Ben Hogan's recent putting woes, to the taste of Claire Hathaway's cunt—the taste of cinnamon and salt.

"What are you thinking about?"

Milmary's voice startled him. He opened one eye and saw that she'd taken off the white blouse and was wearing a black one-piece bathing suit. She was brushing her hair. The coppery highlights flashed in the sun, and her cheekbones jutted sharply. She looked beautiful, yet hard and dangerous.

"I was thinking about what I'm going to say to Marilyn Monroe."

"You mean you get aroused just thinking about her?"

"Hunh?" He propped himself up on one elbow. She was staring at his seersucker swim trunks. He looked down and saw, sure enough, a noticeable bulge.

Now she looked him in the eye. "Is that why you wanted to spend the day out here—so you'll be brown and beautiful when you meet the object of your wildest fantasies?"

"Darling, please don't start."

"I've seen all the clippings and pictures of her you've been saving."

"It so happens we're trying to hire her for a major ad campaign."

"Will she be wearing a bathing suit? Or will she be nude for this one?"

"How many Bloody Marys have you had?"

"Two."

"It's not even noon yet. You celebrating something?"

"As a matter of fact, I am. I finished my story yesterday and sent it off to *The New Yorker*."

"Well . . . congratulations. You haven't even let me read it yet."

"You haven't asked."

"I wasn't sure . . . I didn't know if you wanted anybody to read it."

"You miss everything, don't you?"

"What the hell is that supposed to mean?" He sat up. One of the women on the far side of the pool peeked over the top of her magazine.

"You had no idea I spent the spring and summer writing a story about a pilot during the war. You have no idea that your sons are playing for the Little League championship tomorrow."

"They are?"

"You have no idea that Harvey's Japanese friend is due to arrive tomorrow night—and no clue as to what the poor woman's been through."

"What the hell are you talking about?"

"And you're completely unaware that I haven't had a decent orgasm all summer long."

That did it. He'd come here to unwind, not to get flogged. He stood up, slipped on his shirt, wiggled his feet into his sandals. "Why don't you order some food. Maybe your mood will improve."

"My mood is fine. Where do you think you're going?"

"I'm going down to the driving range to beat the living shit out of some golf balls."

"Oh, that'll solve everything."

"Maybe if you laid off the sauce you'd be able to have a decent orgasm."

"I haven't been drunk in months. Try again."

"Go to hell."

"Oh, that's clever, Teddy. I should've listened to Daddy—he always warned me never to criticize a man for being a lousy driver or a lousy lover. So tell me something—and don't give me any more crap about Marilyn Monroe—what's her name?"

She hadn't planned this, but suddenly there it was, out in the open at last. She looked up at the perfectly combed silver hair, the boiling silver curls on his chest, the sweat wobbling on his brow. He looked menacing, but she drilled him with her stare until he looked away.

"What's whose name?" he hissed, picking up a towel.

"Is it someone at the office?"

"Order some food."

"Someone in the neighborhood?"

"Dammit, Mil—"

"Is it anyone I know? Just tell me who it is, Ted, and I'll forget it ever happened. I deserve to know, goddammit."

"I don't know what you're talking about."

"Jesus, Ted . . ." She pinched the bridge of her nose. She had vowed to herself long ago that when this moment came she would not allow herself to cry. "You know exactly what I'm talking about." She pinched harder, pinched until it hurt. "I'm so tired of living like this."

He flipped the towel over his shoulder and buttoned his shirt. "I'll send a waiter out to take your order. See you in an hour."

He stormed into the clubhouse. At his locker he could barely lace his golf shoes. He realized his hands were not trembling because he was angry; they were trembling because he was terrified.

Though he wouldn't have admitted it to anyone, least of all to himself, Ted Mackey was a desperate man when he arrived at La Guardia Airport. If he could just revive the Wildcat project, he would regain the momentum he'd been losing steadily for months, like a battery draining of juice. And if he could regain his momentum, all of his problems—the design leaks, Plymouth's recent sales surge, the rumblings that he wasn't in control of the ship—would be forgotten.

After checking into his suite at the Plaza, Ted headed straight for Broadway. He wanted to catch Marilyn Monroe on location, before DiMaggio had a chance to get in the way. Ted had learned from Marilyn's manager that she was playing a seductive television model in *The Seven Year Itch*, and he'd read in a recent Hedda Hopper column that DiMaggio, good Sicilian that he was, nearly blacked out with jealousy whenever his wife played such a role. He'd stopped visiting sets and locations where she was working because he couldn't stand to see her, half-dressed and purring, in another man's arms.

Since Ted tended to believe what he read in the tabloids, he was surprised to see DiMaggio on the edge of the mob that had gathered on Broadway. Ted was transfixed by DiMaggio. The Yankee Clipper was taller than Ted had imagined, bulkier through the upper body. He was wearing an expensive camel-hair coat over his dark blue suit, and his silvering hair was perfectly watered and combed. He was beyond glossy, Ted thought. He was radiant. He would have had no trouble fitting in on the fourteenth floor at General Motors headquarters. A dapper little man with a pen and a notebook was standing next to him. DiMaggio was staring straight ahead. Ted noticed his eyes never blinked, and he was constantly clenching and unclenching his jaw.

Then Ted saw why. There Marilyn Monroe was, a pure platinum bombshell, standing over a subway grate on this chilly evening wearing nothing but a white dress and white shoes and a dazzling smile. Her nipples were hard. Every time a train rumbled beneath the grate, her skirt floated up around her waist and she smiled and flashbulbs popped and the crowd roared. She was wearing white panties. She had this crowd on a string, and she loved it. Such power was almost obscene, Ted thought; yet he, like everyone else, was frozen with fascination, physically unable to turn away.

When the bright white lights were shut off and Marilyn stepped off the subway grate, Ted turned toward DiMaggio. He was still staring straight ahead, still working his jaw. Ted moved toward him, but just as he was about to introduce himself he heard DiMaggio mutter to the dapper little man with the notebook, "I've had it, Walter. Let's get the fuck outta here."

Ted watched the two men hurry down Broadway toward Times Square and, no doubt, Toots Shor's. He was delighted to be rid of the jealous husband, but by the time he fought his way through the crowd he was horrified to see Marilyn slipping into a white limousine. He called out to her, but his voice was lost in the roar as the door closed. The driver honked the horn, the crowd slowly parted and the limousine raced into the night.

Ted was furious. He stormed to Toots Shor's and sat alone at the giant circular bar and inhaled two martinis. The only celebrity in the place was Frank Sinatra, who was sitting with his entourage and the proprietor at table 1. Toots kept calling him "Sinat" in a loud, braying voice. Ted left before Toots had a chance to slap him on the back and call him "Theodore."

From a pay phone at Columbus Circle he called the St.

Regis. But the operator told him she was under instructions to hold all of the DiMaggios' calls. On his way to the hotel, Ted stopped twice more for martinis. The gin helped burn away his rage but did little to bolster his confidence. What had started out as a simple, clear-cut mission had suddenly become a minefield. When he finally made it into the lobby, he realized he was weaving. He squinted under the bright lights. The receptionist gave him a frosty look.

"Could you ring the DiMaggios for me, please?" he said. "Suite seven-eighteen."

"I'm sorry, sir, they've asked me to hold all calls. Would you like to leave a message?"

"No. I need to speak with them right now. Tell them Ted Mackey—M-a-c-k-e-y—is here from General Motors. They're expecting me."

"Sir, I'm sorry. Those were strict orders from Mr. DiMaggio."

"'S'okay. I'll wait."

He sat on one of the sofas by the fireplace. A fire was burning heartily, and it cheered him, chased the chill from his bones. But after an hour of pretending to read a magazine he began to feel foolish, like some groveling fan hoping for a glimpse of his idol. He realized there were half a dozen other people in the lobby pretending to read magazines, including the dapper little man who'd been with DiMaggio on Broadway.

How, Ted asked himself, had the general manager of the Buick Division been reduced to lurking in a hotel lobby hoping desperately for a word with a movie actress? As he stood up to leave, he noticed the elevator attendant and a bellhop looking at him, whispering to one another. Spinning through the revolving door, he thought he heard them laughing.

On the flight back to Detroit the next morning, Ted Mackey read Louella Parsons's account of the "sparks" that had flown on the movie set between Marilyn Monroe and Joe DiMaggio. "The combat continued in their suite at the St. Regis," Parsons wrote, "but the hotel staff refused to give a damage estimate. Perhaps the best way to tally the damage is simply to report that DiMaggio left late last night for California, and it's no longer a secret that America's favorite fairytale marriage is on the rocks.''

Ted spent the rest of the flight drinking scotch and getting used to the fact that the Wildcat was a goner.

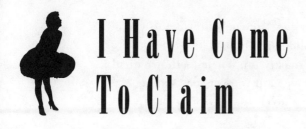

I Have Come To Claim

Judy Grahn

I have come to claim
Marilyn Monroe's body
for the sake of my own.
dig it up, hand it over,
cram it in this paper sack.
hubba. hubba. hubba.
look at those luscious
long brown bones, that wide and crusty
pelvis. ha HA, oh she wanted so much to be serious

but she never stops smiling now.
Has she lost her mind?

Marilyn, be serious—they're taking
your picture, and they're taking the pictures
of eight young women in New York City
who murdered themselves for being pretty
by the same method as you, the very
next day, after you!
I have claimed their bodies too,
they smile up out of my paper sack
like brainless cinderellas.

the reporters are furious, they're asking
me questions
what right does a woman have

to Marilyn Monroe's body? and what
am I doing for lunch? They think I
mean to eat you. Their teeth are lurid
and they want to pose me, leaning
on the shovel, nude. Dont squint.

But when one of the reporters comes too close
I beat him, bust his camera
with your long, smooth thigh
and with your lovely knucklebone
I break his eye.

Long ago you wanted to write poems;
Be serious, Marilyn
I am going to take you in this paper sack
around the world, and
write on it:—the poems of Marilyn Monroe—
Dedicated to all princes,
the male poets who were so sorry to see you go,
before they had a crack at you.
They wept for you, and also
they wanted to stuff you
while you still had a little meat left
in useful places;
but they were too slow.

Now I shall take them my paper sack
and we shall act out a poem together:
"How would you like to see Marilyn Monroe,
in action, smiling, and without her clothes?"
We shall wait long enough to see them make
      familiar faces
and then I shall beat them with your skull.
hubba. hubba. hubba. hubba. hubba.
Marilyn, be serious
Today I have come to claim your body for my
      own.

FROM Son of Celluloid

Clive Barker

Ricky sat in the flickering light and examined his sanity. If Birdy said the boy wasn't in there, then presumably she was telling the truth. The best way to verify that was to see for himself. Then he'd be certain he'd suffered a minor reality crisis brought on by some bad dope, and he'd go home, lay his head down to sleep and wake tomorrow afternoon healed. Except that he didn't want to put his head in that evil-smelling room. Suppose she was wrong, and *she* was the one having the crisis? Weren't there such things as hallucinations of normality?

Shakily, he hauled himself up, crossed the aisle and pushed open the door. It was murky inside, but he could see enough to know that there were no sandstorms, or dead boys, no gun-toting cowboys, nor even a solitary tumbleweed. It's quite a thing, he thought, this mind of mine. To have created an alternative world so eerily well. It was a wonderful trick. Pity it couldn't be turned to better use than scaring him shitless. You win some, you lose some.

And then he saw the blood. On the tiles. A smear of blood that hadn't come from his nicked ear, there was too much of it. Ha! He didn't imagine it at all. There was blood, heel marks, every sign that what he thought he'd seen, he'd seen. But Jesus in Heaven, which was worse? To see, or not to see? Wouldn't it have been better to be wrong, and just a little spaced-out tonight, than right, and in the hands of a power that could literally change the world?

Ricky stared at the trail of blood, and followed it across

the floor of the toilet to the cubicle on the left of his vision. Its door was closed: it had been open before. The murderer, whoever he was, had put the boy in there, Ricky knew it without looking.

"O.K.," he said, "now I've got you."

He pushed on the door. It swung open and there was the boy, propped up on the toilet seat, legs spread, arms hanging.

His eyes had been scooped out of his head. Not neatly: no surgeon's job. They'd been wrenched out, leaving a trail of mechanics down his cheek.

Ricky put his hand over his mouth and told himself he wasn't going to throw up. His stomach churned, but obeyed, and he ran to the toilet door as though any moment the body was going to get up and demand its ticket-money back.

"Birdy . . . Birdy . . ."

The fat bitch had been wrong, all wrong. There was death here, and worse.

Ricky flung himself out of the john into the body of the cinema.

The wall lights were fairly dancing behind their Deco shades, guttering like candles on the verge of extinction. Darkness would be too much; he'd lose his mind.

There was, it occurred to him, something familiar about the way the lights flickered, something he couldn't quite put his finger on. He stood in the aisle for a moment, hopelessly lost.

Then the voice came; and though he guessed it was death this time, he looked up.

"Hello Ricky," she was saying as she came along Row E towards him. Not Birdy. No, Birdy never wore a white gossamer dress, never had bruisefull lips, or hair so fine, or eyes so sweetly promising. It was Monroe who was walking towards him, the blasted rose of America.

"Aren't you going to say hello?" she gently chided.

". . . er . . ."

"Ricky. Ricky. Ricky. After all this time."

All this time? What did she mean: all this time?

"Who are you?"

She smiled radiantly at him.

"As if you didn't know."

"You're not Marilyn. Marilyn's dead."

"Nobody dies in the movies, Ricky. You know that as well as I do. You can always thread the celluloid up again—"

—that was what the flickering reminded him of, the flicker of celluloid through the gate of a projector, one image hot on the next, the illusion of life created from a perfect sequence of little deaths.

"—and we're there again, all talking, all singing." She laughed: ice-in-a-glass laughter, "We never fluff our lines, never age, never lose our timing—"

"You're not real," said Ricky.

She looked faintly bored by the observation, as if he was being pedantic.

By now she'd come to the end of the row and was standing no more than three feet away from him. At this distance the illusion was as ravishing and as complete as ever. He suddenly wanted to take her, there, in the aisle. What the hell if she was just a fiction: fictions are fuckable if you don't want marriage.

"I want you," he said, surprised by his own bluntness.

"I want *you*," she replied, which surprised him even more. "In fact I need you. I'm very weak."

"Weak?"

"It's not easy, being the center of attraction, you know. You find you need it, more and more. Need people to look at you. All the night, all the day."

"I'm looking."

"Am I beautiful?"

"You're a goddess: whoever you are."

"I'm yours: that's who I am."

It was a perfect answer. She was defining herself through him. I am a function of you; made for you, out of you. The perfect fantasy.

"Keep looking at me; looking *forever*, Ricky. I need your loving looks. I can't live without them."

The more he stared at her the stronger her image seemed to become. The flickering had almost stopped; a calm had settled over the place.

"Do you want to touch me?"

He thought she'd never ask.

"Yes," he said.

"Good." She smiled coaxingly at him, and he reached to make contact. She elegantly avoided his fingertips at the last possible moment, and ran, laughing, down the aisle towards the screen. He followed, eager. She wanted a game: that was fine by him.

She'd run into a cul-de-sac. There was no way out from this end of the cinema, and judging by the come-ons she was giving him, she knew it. She turned and flattened herself against the wall, feet spread a little.

He was within a couple of yards of her when a breeze out of nowhere billowed her skirt up around her waist. She laughed, half closing her eyes, as the surf of silk rose and exposed her. She was naked underneath.

Ricky reached for her again and this time she didn't avoid his touch. The dress billowed up a little higher and he stared, fixated, at the part of Marilyn he had never seen, the fur divide that had been the dream of millions.

There was blood there. Not much, a few fingermarks on her inner thighs. The faultless gloss of her flesh was spoiled slightly. Still he stared; and the lips parted a little as she moved her hips, and he realized the glint of wetness in her interior was not the juice of her body, but something else altogether. As her muscles moved the bloody eyes she'd buried in her body shifted, and came to rest on him.

She knew by the look on his face that she hadn't hidden them deep enough, but where was a girl with barely a veil of cloth covering her nakedness to hide the fruits of her labor?

"You killed him," said Ricky, still looking at the lips, and the eyes that peeked out between. The image was so engrossing, so pristine, it all but canceled out the horror in his belly. Perversely, his disgust fed his lust instead of killing it. So what if she *was* a murderer: she was legend.

"Love me," she said. "Love me forever."

He came to her, knowing now full well that it was death to do so. But death was a relative matter, wasn't it? Marilyn was dead in the flesh, but alive here, either in his brain, or in the buzzing matrix of the air or both; and he could be with her.

He embraced her, and she him. They kissed. It was easy. Her lips were softer than he'd imagined, and he felt something close to pain at his crotch; he wanted to be in her so much.

The willow-thin arms slipped around his waist, and he was in the lap of luxury.

"You make me strong," she said. "Looking at me that way. I need to be looked at, or I die. It's the natural state of illusions."

Her embrace was tightening; the arms at his back no longer seemed quite so willowlike. He struggled a little against the discomfort.

"No use," she cooed in his ear. "You're mine."

He wrenched his head around to look at her grip and to his amazement the arms weren't arms any longer, just a loop of something round his back, without hands or fingers or wrists.

"Jesus Christ!" he said.

"Look at me, boy," she said. The words had lost their delicacy. It wasn't Marilyn that had him in its arms anymore: nothing like her. The embrace tightened again, and the breath was forced from Ricky's body, breath the tightness of the hold prevented him from recapturing. His spine creaked under the pressure, and pain shot through his body like flares, exploding in his eyes, all colors.

"You should have got out of town," said Marilyn, as Wayne's face blossomed under the sweep of her perfect cheek-bones. His look was contemptuous, but Ricky had only a moment to register it before that image cracked too, and something else came into focus behind this façade of famous faces. For the last time in his life, Ricky asked the question:

"Who are you?"

His captor didn't answer. It was feeding on his fascination; even as he stared twin organs erupted out of its body like the horns of a slug, antennae perhaps, forming themselves into probes and crossing the space between its head and Ricky's.

"I need you," it said, its voice now neither Wayne nor Monroe, but a crude, uncultivated voice, a thug's voice. "I'm so fucking weak; it uses me up, being in the world."

It was mainlining on him, feeding itself, whatever it was, on his stares, once adoring—now horrified. He could feel it draining out his life through his eyes, luxuriating in the soul looks he was giving it as he perished.

He knew he must be nearly dead, because he hadn't taken a breath in a long while. It seemed like minutes, but he couldn't be sure.

Just as he was listening for the sound of his heart, the horns divided around his head and pressed themselves into his ears. Even in this reverie, the sensation was disgusting, and he wanted to cry out for it to stop. But the fingers were working their way into his head, bursting his eardrums, and passing on like inquisitive tapeworms through brain and skull. He was alive, even now, still staring at his tormentor, and he knew that the fingers were finding his eyeballs, and pressing on them now from behind.

His eyes bulged suddenly and broke from their housing, splashing from his sockets. Momentarily he saw the world from a different angle as his sense of sight cascaded down his cheek. There was his lip, his chin—

It was an appalling experience, and mercifully short. Then the feature Ricky'd lived for thirty-seven years snapped in mid-reel, and he slumped in the arms of fiction.

FROM Marilyn's Daughter

John Rechy

The plan was concocted at first only to allow Marilyn Monroe hope that she might be able to have the child she wanted more than anything else in her life—and at the same time to stave off the threatened scandal such a child would enflame for the dynasty of the Kennedys. It pitted two archenemies, Alberta Holland and Mildred Meadows, against each other.

Enid Morgan had just returned from Texas, where she had gone, she said in her cryptic, cynical way, to have "the child of a son of a bitch." Soon after, Mildred's rampage on Marilyn Monroe occurred. Enid knew they must turn to Alberta Holland. She admired the staunch counselor, and Marilyn "loved" her.

Sipping her fragrant tea, Alberta Holland listened to the reason for the visit of the two beautiful women. "Is the asserted involvement with the Kennedys—both of them—true?"

"Yes," Marilyn answered. She looked defiantly at Enid.

Alberta tempered her voice to soothe her words. "I'm sorry to agree that Mildred is right, in that a pregnancy discovered or a child born amid inflammatory accusations will implicate the brothers, one or both, and perhaps . . . destroy them." And with them would be crushed the inspired dream she championed, of a social Camelot, she thought but did not say.

"Nothing must harm Robert! Or *Mr.* President." Marilyn said the last with only a touch of resentment. "They mustn't even *know* any*thing about *any* of this. And you both must promise me. Please promise me now!''

Alberta promised, touched. Her cigarette lighter dormant in her hands, Enid nodded her agreement.

Marilyn's voice diminished. ''I still love Robert, and I want this child.''

What Alberta had heard bruised her feelings about the Kennedys. She knew it is possible for men to be great leaders yet flawed in their private lives. Her second-favorite writer, Shakespeare—she preferred Proust—had dealt with just that. . . . So she did not judge. She had adored Marilyn Monroe from their first encounter—admired her intelligence, sensitivity, daring. Yet there was a distinct vulnerability about her that might cause her to misjudge intentions, perceive— *hope* for—commitment where none had been offered, perhaps not even implied. She knew, too, that if the Kennedys fell— with the symbolic power of a longed-for ''new frontier''—the country would reel in reaction. Among others, Richard Nixon waited greedily. The good the Kennedys symbolized must be protected.

Alberta Holland had a reputation for being a profoundly, even blindly, earnest woman of dedication. According to her trusted friend, Teresa de Pilar, ''the indomitable Alberta'' had once claimed, ''Smiling is frivolous when injustice is rampant.'' Still, she smiled fondly now at Marilyn. Borrowing a phrase the two women had used earlier, she promised, ''You *will* have your child, perhaps in an interval of lavender spring which will occur just for you.''

Then Alberta's mind tumbled furiously as she began to shape her plan: ''Mildred must be tricked into using the offered item about a miscarriage, a reconciliation with a loving ex-husband.'' The brothers would survive the remains of the threatened scandal, she told them. Robbed of the enormous impact of Marilyn's name—and of the pregnancy—it would all become just gossip, accusations all men of power endure, rumors without evidence. ''Rumors capable of arousing sympathy,'' she added, and hoped that that would be so. ''The item in Mildred's column has to be false, but believed.''

''That's very smart. Yes, that's what we have to do!'' Marilyn was desperate to accept a firm solution.

Enid said with a wry smile, "Of course it is. But how are you going to make Mildred cooperate, Alberta?"

"By cunning, duplicity, lies—*her* terms." Through years of mutual detestation, she and Mildred had come to know each other intimately. They watched each other from a distance, read everything about each other.

Eager to be reassured, Marilyn let her attention wander away from the web of dangers, out the window, to peaceful breaths of lavender outside. She wished none of this were happening. She imagined that there would be the sudden eager honking of a car outside, and it would be Robert. She imagined their conversation. He would begin, "I love you—"

"Once the item appears"—Alberta's mind was sweeping over all her knowledge of the detested woman—"Mildred won't dare retract it. She'll separate herself from even defused scandal. To do otherwise would mean admitting that she—*Mildred Mead*-ows!"—she shredded the name—"has been duped, deceived, fooled"—she embraced each word—"*and* by Alberta Holland!" Again, she hoped she was right.

Even as Alberta's mind continued to toss with ideas, she studied the two women closely. They at first appeared to be opposites because of the difference in their hair coloring, their manner: Enid was dark-haired, cool, somewhat aloof; Marilyn was blond, warm, openly affectionate. In that careful scrutiny, Alberta detected a natural beauty in Enid that Marilyn had copied—no, *created*, Alberta withdrew any implicit judgment in her assessment—created through masterful artifice that had now achieved its own reality, its *own* naturalness.

Enid must have understood the meaningful, careful attention to their appearance, because she offered this information: For years—"to confuse reporters for the hell of it and give Marilyn some privacy"—Enid had often appeared in public, not as Marilyn Monroe but as "Marilyn Monroe in disguise." One or the other of them would tip eager reporters: "Wearing a black wig, Marilyn will be at ——— , on ——— , dressed in ———." When photographers sprang at her, Enid would shelter her face, just so, while making sure it was captured by the cameras. That image became so recognizable that several times her photograph appeared identified as "Marilyn

Monroe spotted in her usual disguise." To lock the masquerade, during one daring and rare excursion together—

"*I* wore a black wig and was Enid, and Enid wore a blond wig and was *me*; and *she* was asked for autographs while *I* was ignored." Marilyn joined in with the sudden delight of a schoolgirl.

Her eyes holding Alberta's tightening scrutiny, Enid went on to tell about her best performance as Marilyn, a time when she'd recognized Mildred Meadows spying from her limousine while her photographer pursued with clicking camera. "I deliberately backed up against her ugly car—a car I'll never forget," she added with a shudder of memory—and her look on Marilyn shared it. "I was so close that I saw her white face behind the dark pane."

Alberta knew how possible their subterfuge was. There was a unique "sameness" beyond appearance and similar outline. It must come out of an intense association, known only to them. An idea gained strength. Later, Alberta would wonder to what extent Enid had helped to guide it.

"So Mildred still has the picture," Alberta said to herself. During silenced moments, she freshened their tea. She brought out a few more of the plump little madeleine cakes she so enjoyed. As she sipped her tea and took a bite of her little cake, Alberta searched for an essential connection—it was already lurking!—from a distant time she had shared with Mildred, a connection to present circumstances. Now she roamed through that time:

Mildred had had a consuming closeness with her exquisitely beautiful daughter, Tarah. When Tarah became pregnant by an actor, a drifter, Mildred contacted him and suggested a meeting to explore "matters of mutual benefit." At her invitation, they met in her greenhouse—"where we will be assured of privacy"—at the exact time of day that Tarah tended to her rare orchids, a hobby Mildred encouraged. Separated from Tarah by lush vines, Mildred met with the actor, the drifter. She offered him a large amount of money to exit from her daughter's life. He eagerly accepted. Mildred turned to Tarah, who had heard every word just as Mildred had intended. "He didn't even barter for more," Mildred disdained. The drifter got nothing, not a cent. Tarah rejected him with a ferocity Mildred complimented at dinner that night—a celebratory dinner of lobster with the lightest butter sauce and an astonishing Dom Perignon.

Mildred stopped delighting in the evening when Tarah informed her that she intended to have her child. "You'll destroy your whole life, your reputation, your beauty!" Mildred appealed to logic.

Some time after, Mildred "eerily acquiesced" to the birth. Gaily, she informed Tarah that she had arranged for the child to be born "under the most careful circumstances, and, of course, at the D'Arcy House, under the care of that most trusted Dr. Janus." Afraid, Tarah turned to the one person beyond reach of her mother's arteries of power—Alberta Holland. Alberta agreed to contact Dr. Janus, to assure that all was right. Of course it was not. Mildred had been emphatic with Dr. Janus that a stillborn child would be "vastly appreciated and equally rewarded." Alberta "convinced" the doctor that if he did not reject the terrifying proposition, *she* would assure him prison.

With Mildred in chilling attendance in the amber-hued room at the D'Arcy House, Tarah gave birth to a live child. Dr. Janus held it out to Mildred, who turned away in disgust. Five years later, driving away in a rage from Mildred's increasing rampages against the child's "ugliness," Tarah crashed in her car. Mildred blamed the death of Tarah on the child, insisting her daughter was always protecting "the ugly little creature," who, it was true, nestled in fear against her mother at every moment. . . . That violence in Mildred's past provided a strong undertow to her demands on Marilyn.

Alberta popped another madeleine into her mouth. Suddenly she knew how she would use that sad, ugly incident to protect Marilyn *and* her child. "We have to convince Mildred that she has *seen* the demanded abortion!"

Enid held her lighter tensely.

"I couldn't simulate—" Marilyn shivered with horror.

"Of course not," Alberta reassured her tenderly.

Now Alberta's plan formed—so daring, so audacious that it *would* work. In a few hours, at Mildred's mansion, as demanded, Enid would inform Mildred that Marilyn had—of course—acquiesced to her "logical demands." "Mildred believes in the irrefutable logic of evil," Alberta explained. Enid would provide the woman with all the information on how her insane demand would be carried out, identifying the place of execution—"'the D'Arcy House, of course'"; she would agree to verify the exact date and time later.

"You must keep saying 'of course' in order to plant suspicion," Alberta advised Enid. Enid would then inform Mildred that Marilyn must be in disguise—of course. "Then," Alberta instructed Enid, "you must add, very, very quickly, that the disguise will be one she's familiar with—say it as if to assuage her—a disguise one of her photographers captured on film while she oversaw from her limousine. When she—"

"I wish—" Marilyn sighed. Her own fantasy fought her. It had stopped as Robert was about to introduce her to his mother. Marilyn stood up. "I feel suddenly sad. You and Enid talk, please, and tell me all you said, later." She placed an appreciative hand on Alberta's shoulder. "I'd like to lie in the sun."

But there was no sun.

How alone she seemed, hoping for sun on an increasingly graying day, Alberta thought, placing her own hand over Marilyn's. For a moment she allowed herself to imagine that she had a daughter, that her daughter was Marilyn.

Marilyn called a cab. She would wait outside, she said, to allow them to continue talking. At the door she turned around, all curves and blond beauty and outrageous sensuality, and breathed a puff of gratitude: "And *thank* you, thank you a whole lot, *really*," she told Alberta.

The gray day turned silver. Alberta imagined Marilyn Monroe standing outside studying the lavender blossoms that fascinated her. Yes, they were like her in that they, too, had a special beauty. But they lasted so briefly; Alberta did not welcome that thought.

Alberta directed her attention back to Enid—startled anew by Enid's cooler beauty. "Mildred will—" But she had lost her train of thought in the bedazzled moments.

Enid guided her back knowledgeably: "You want me to guide Mildred to the photograph by her limousine."

"Yes!" Then Alberta conveyed her evolving plan to Enid, "with embellishments to be supplied as required." It relied on stirring in Mildred a calculated series of associations and suspicions. From that time when the haunting young woman had sought her help, Alberta remembered being fascinated by Tarah's unique mannerisms, the perfection of manners demanded by Mildred in constant quiet war with a desire to rebel against such imposed rigidity. This resulted in quick but graceful movements, as if ceremony must be gotten out of the way: sudden attention to her makeup at odd moments; a soft lifting of the veil of her hat to reveal a new expression. She said "please" often, while her eyes flashed in rejection of pleading. She had asked Alberta whether she might have some sherry—"just three sips," she'd added automatically, then instantly rejected her own request, explaining that Mildred had come to expect those exact words from her, uttered first when she was only a girl and now cherished as part of a ritual, while they waited for dusk, to watch Mildred's garden change its shadings.

As Alberta spoke those memories of Tarah, Enid listened attentively, as if already rehearsing what Alberta was only now revealing.

"By suggesting those movements, using a few key words, you must arouse in Mildred her memory of the daughter she destroyed while claiming to love her." Alberta explained to Enid the horrible parallel between Mildred's unsuccessful demand on Tarah and the present one on Marilyn. They would use that to their own ends.

Alberta continued to explain: After Enid left the mansion of the hated woman, Mildred would suspect everything that had occurred between them. She always did, believing that one uncovered truth only by discovering lies. She would realize that Enid had *intended* to guide her to a certain photograph of Marilyn Monroe, to verify the disguise to be employed at the D'Arcy House. She would discover what they wanted her to—that the photograph was of Enid pretending to be Monroe in a dark wig.

Alberta was certain of this: Mildred would then couple her discovery with Enid's admonishment that she, Mildred, would—of course—not be allowed into the guarded house. She would make the desired conclusion: They *wanted* her there, carrying in her mind the cleverly implanted image in the photograph, the same image she would see at the D'Arcy House in a grandly simulated abortion.

"She will be sure it will be me pretending to be Marilyn," Enid understood, "but it won't be."

"Exactly." When Mildred entered the D'Arcy House, Alberta continued with the excitement of a general about to vanquish another with impeccable strategy based on perfect knowledge of the enemy's own maneuvers, the systematic disorientation of Mildred, already prepared for, would immediately commence. The time would be set for a certain phase of twilight when visual perception is almost equivocal. From the elaborate windows of the D'Arcy House, refracted shards of light, colored by the stained glass, would slice at Mildred's eyes. Simultaneously, her confidence would grow as she encountered predictable obstacles—guards, attendants she would accept, thrilled, as part of the charade staged to deceive her. At the exact moment, Enid would run out of a certain room. Mildred's assumptions would crash. She would be forced into the only conclusion that would not prove her deductions wrong: At the last moment Enid had faced the impossibility of the contrived deceit and so had fled.

But—

When Mildred opened the room she would be triumphantly certain she would find vacated with only the instruments of the simulated operation remaining in judgment of foiled cunning, she would be pitched into a turmoil of memories by a graphic unexpected sight: In the same amber-hued room in which Tarah's child had been born, she would see a doctor she vaguely recognized, extending to her the mangled proof of the demanded abortion. In shattered moments of jarred perception, images of Tarah in childbirth, Tarah dying, Monroe in the demanded abortion once demanded of Tarah would tangle violently—Tarah, Monroe, Tarah, Monroe, Tarah—Rejecting the unmistakable pursuing face of memory, she would be forced to grasp defensively for that of present reality, convincing herself she had seen Marilyn Monroe.

Enid leaned away from the eerie confidence with which Alberta predicted the expertly manipulated confusion of images that would lead Mildred to the required conclusion.

"But Mildred will have seen *another* woman in the *simulated* abortion?" Enid spoke slowly, precisely, but she had not intended to form a question.

"What else?" Alberta said tersely.

With sustained care in her choice of words, Enid said, "It's all possible, Alberta. I agree that Mildred would be thrown into the terrible confusion your brilliant plan requires, but not by a simulated abortion." She held her eyes on Alberta's.

"Then we'll have to convince her that it *isn't* simulated." Alberta drank her tea.

Enid felt a cold apprehension, because when she spoke those last words, Alberta Holland, for the first time in their conversation, avoided her eyes.

Something's Got To Give

David Trinidad

A sliver of light below the locked door
alerted Mrs. Murray (the live-in
hired by Monroe's psychiatrist, Doctor
Greenson) to the grim fact that Marilyn
was still awake. It was 3 A.M. She'd
yet to shake the case of sinusitis
that had forced her—though she wished to proceed
with the film under way at Fox—to miss
a week of principal photography.
Twice she'd dragged herself to the lot, only
to faint beneath the blazing lights. Now she
lay between satin sheets—restless, lonely
and drenched with sweat. She reached for the phone. Her
insomnia was her nightly terror.

Insomnia was her nightly terror
so she gulped "bedtime cocktails": Nembutal
dissolved in champagne. Often this mixture
failed to knock her out and it would be followed by handfuls of pills. She was always
late; sometimes she arrived on the soundstage
too puffy for close-ups. "She's drugged and dazed,"
George Cukor told the press. "It's an outrage."
The director had come to hate the star
when they made *Let's Make Love*. They had finished
only a few scenes for the new picture
and were nine days behind schedule. Against

his protests, Marilyn walked off the set
and flew to New York in a private jet.

She flew to New York in a private jet
with her soon-to-be-famous "Tinseltown
dress," which she had paid Jean Louis, her pet
designer, twelve grand to create. The gown
was made of "silk soufflé," the lightest and
sheerest fabric in the world, and covered
with more than six thousand shimmering hand-
sewn beads. Her scarf hid her sizzling new hair
color—a tint *Vogue* would dub "pillow slip
white." Stark naked, she'd be stitched into her
dress the following night. She'd slither up
to the microphone, squirm out of her fur
wrap, and breathlessly sing "Happy Birthday"
to her top secret lover, JFK.

Her top secret affair with JFK
ended abruptly after the gala
at Madison Square Garden. Without saying why, Jack just dropped her. Monroe caught a
plane back to L.A., where she sequestered
herself in her bedroom, guzzling more bar-
biturate-spiked bubbly. She recovered
by staging a stunt that no other star
would have dared. She made sure photographers
were on hand for her sexy "skinny-dip"
sequence. As she splashed in the water, their
Nikons flashed. Then, "by accident," she slipped
off her flesh-toned mesh bikini. Bedlam
broke loose when, nude, she continued to swim.

As photos of Marilyn's "midnight swim"
bumped Liz's face off countless magazine
covers, Bobby delivered a solemn
message from "the Prez": "It's over between
us. Stop calling the White House." Then he wooed
her right into bed. Later the actress
confided to friends that both brothers screwed

like adolescents—"in and out in less
than a minute." Meanwhile, the film progressed
by fits. After a strained birthday party,
she left the set for the last time. Distressed
by what Cukor described as a "zombie-
like performance" and "deranged behavior,"
the studio decided to fire her.

When Fox officially dismissed her, her
staunch co-star stood firm: NO MM, NO DEAN
MARTIN, read the *Herald Examiner's*
banner headline. Drunk on wine, Monroe leaned
against the balcony of Peter and
Pat Lawford's beachfront mansion, dispirit-
edly toasting the blizzard of white sand
stirred up by Bobby's chopper. Their visit
had gone badly. Unlike Jack, he had talked
marriage; he'd lied to her, then tried to cut
her loose. As she rambled, Lawford uncorked
a fresh bottle. She'd been passed like a slut
from one to the other, so now she planned
to blow the lid off the Kennedy clan.

Alarmed, Lawford called the Kennedy clan
and warned them of Marilyn's threat. From her
bedroom window, she watched a repair van
parked on the street. Convinced the Secret Service had bugged her line (she heard clicks every
time she talked), she'd often lug a purseful
of coins to a phone booth, her diary
(loaded with proof of her political
trysts) tucked under her arm. This document
disappeared after her alleged OD.
According to Mrs. Murray, who sent
for the ambulance, she felt uneasy
when she noticed, in the dark corridor,
a sliver of light below the locked door.

Waiting to See

L. A. Lantz

I'm standing in our kitchen. I'm fourteen, but quite naive, as girls could be when raised in the suburbs of Philadelphia just before the real sixties hit. My mother's hand quivers as she pours milk into a blue wavy glass for me. She says, "I cannot allow this." Her skin almost ripples with anger. She wears a yellow dress that almost matches her kitchen curtains. The folds of both stand out sharply because she believes that starch is a necessary part of the diet like multivitamins. My father leans on the doorjamb, drawn away from his beloved television. It glows uneven blue from the living room. My father's a quiet man. He looks very like his photos from when he was younger, except balder, and I think that makes him quieter. Now, though, he has a slight smile on his face—I've seen that smile before.

"What can you do about it?" he says.

"Nothing," he adds. My mother stares.

"You wait and see," she says archly and goes to their room. My father and I return to the television. We don't talk because we're waiting to see what we're waiting to see.

Since that night I've seen it on television so many times that I can't really remember how I saw it the first time. I think it was on the late news. And I think my father called my mother in, excitedly, and I wonder if he regretted that act of revenge. The woman I saw on the stage swayed taller, and more voluptuous, and sultry than she even was. Her dress was skintight and sequined in very special spots. When she sang "Happy Birthday," her voice curled out like smoke over the stage and wrapped its arms around the President sitting in the front row of the audience with that characteristic folded-arm thing. My mother had said before that he looked very thoughtful that way, but at the time I thought he looked embarrassed. My mother walked right up on the screen, peering at its gray edges, into the darkness of the crowd around the stage.

"Evelyn," said my father, "move, you're in the way." She jerked upright. "I'm looking for poor Jacqueline. That poor woman." Marilyn rocked slightly and some of the words to the song were fuzzy, as if she'd just awakened from a long, satisfying sleep. She gave my stomach a jolt like she was something I shouldn't be watching, but I wanted to. My mother must've thought so too because she suddenly pulled me off to the kitchen, holding my wrist too tightly.

The next day my mother doesn't make breakfast for my father. He comes into the kitchen, eager to make up, and then looks around like he's wandered into someone else's house by mistake. He sits at the kitchen table for a little while and watches the cupboards, but I don't think he knows where anything is in there so I take pity on him and make him some Cheerios. I see my mother sitting in the living room and I imagine that she's listening to what we say, but we still don't talk. We're waiting. Finally she calls in, "Lucy, you ask your father if he likes this new way of life, because that's what he's going to get when the family structure collapses because of that immoral woman."

My mother marches into Mr. Craig's drugstore like she's the blitzkrieg. I'm hoping this is one of those times when children shouldn't be present, but she calls to me from the magazine rack.

Mr. Craig asks, "Mrs. Kramer, what can I do for you today?"

"Mr. Craig, I'm not saying this is your fault because I myself did not know the scope of the situation until yesterday."

"Scope?" he echoes, glancing at me, smile waning, but I'm leafing through a copy of *Life*. Ignoring them both.

"Marilyn Monroe." She picks up a copy of *Photoplay*, "She is featured in this magazine and also in these gossip magazines.

"She's a very poor role model for the children who come in here, like Lucy." Saying this, she whips the *Life* magazine back on the shelf and leaves me standing there slump-shouldered. "I want you to return these to your publishers and inform them that this type of filth does not belong in the shops of decent American citizens." She extends two stacks of magazines to Mr. Craig, who smiles at her the same way he smiles at the retarded kid who collects for the newspaper.

"I don't know but what you've got a real bee in your bonnet. People do have the right to read what they want."

My mother frowns steadily, then she hands me a stack of magazines and guides me quickly to the door.

"Run for the car!" she shrieks suddenly.

"Now, Mrs. Kramer," he calls out to us, with his arms crossed in that embarrassed way, "What d'you want to do that for? It's stealing."

She locks her car door and rolls down the window, "Mr. Craig, you haven't seen the last of me."

My mother has lost her mind. I slide down low in the seat.

My mother hits a few other drugstores with remarkably similar results, then we whip over to the train station where she drops Daddy in the morning. The person who manages the newsstand is a woman. My mother tells me to stay put by the door and walks over to talk to her. I've never been in the station. A voice over the intercom announces the 12:15 to New York City making stops at Philadelphia, Dover, Trenton, Princeton, and Newark. What would it be like to cross that platform through the smoke and noise and travel to a place where a woman in sequins could shimmy to her president. Call him Jack maybe.

My mother grabs my arm and pulls me to the car, "Oh, Lucy, I am sad to say this. You will discover that there are people who do not recognize John F. Kennedy as the great leader of this country. The only man who can take our young country safely on to the center stage where we Americans belong." She searches in her purse for a Kleenex before driving us home.

* * *

When my father changes from his suit, he says that Mr. Craig and Mr. Bettenham called at the office to complain.

My mother switches off the KitchenAid mixer and faces him. I keep slicing tomatoes a quarter of an inch thick.

"What did you say?" Her voice shakes. He looks at the partially mashed potatoes. The Crisco in the frying pan spits and pops around three pork chops.

He hesitates. "I told them to talk to you. I'm not your parent."

"Thank you," says Mother. She turns the mixer back on and says loudly, "I had a horrible day. They just don't see that the common man is necessary to democracy."

He sits at the table and all but puts his head in his hands. He is, after all, the one who kept telling her that he'd heard someone in his office say that his brother, a reporter, knew that the great John F. Kennedy would chase anything in anything remotely resembling a skirt. She had defended her hero steadfastly, but only in the privacy of our home, until now.

Who is this Marilyn Monroe that she can change my mother, the President, and maybe, if Mother is right, the country? My mother loses weight. Her hands shake sometimes; she says, "Lucy, I want you to go through your father's jackets while I look through his pants." I take all of my father's suit jackets from the closet and lay them on the bed. From his pants pockets I retrieve spearmint Life Savers and his good fountain pen that he was looking for the night before last. I slide what change I find in the pockets of my shorts.

"Mother," I ask finally, "what am I looking for?"

She looks confused. Either she does not want to tell me or she thought that I knew implicitly what she wanted.

"Evidence."

"Of what?"

"Oh, Lucy," she says, exasperated, so that a few bits of saliva squeeze out of the side of her mouth, "of an affair."

"Daddy?" I say. My stomach does a few flips. "Mother, Daddy is not having an affair. Daddy is not the President."

70

"I know that," she answers sharply, but she sits on the edge of the bed.

"No, I mean, just because the President is seeing Marilyn Monroe . . ."

"Don't say that name in my house!"

"Daddy is not having an affair."

"How do you know? This country is in serious trouble and I'm afraid that your father could be at the tip of the iceberg. I see that young family in the White House and I knew as soon as I saw him run for office that he had the interests of the country at heart. He holds our fate in his hand and now, now I don't know. How does your father know what the President is up to? Just go through his things. You're really too young to understand."

This is not my mother.

When we finish, finding nothing, she sits on the scratchy blue couch in front of the TV as if that would teach her more about my father or the President.

My mother goes to the PTA. She bakes cookies. She vacuums every day and switches her houseplants to bigger pots every six months.

She calls to me, "Lucy, put on the water for egg noodles and open a can of tuna," but she doesn't leave the living room until my father calls from the train station promptly at 6:00 P.M., as he does every single workday of his life. I'm not required to search his clothing again.

I write to Fox Studio six times for photos of Marilyn. Because it's summer, I can sit on the front step and wait for the postman. I tape my photos to the inside of my closet door. I'm not sure why one won't suffice. They all appear to be the same. After I receive the fourth one, I sneak the step stool and I begin to retape the photos from the top of the closet door. The studio writes me that fans aren't allowed to have more than three photos of Marilyn. A magic number?

For a week this stops me, but then I roam the neighborhood, looking for other children. If they will send this letter to this address and return the photo to me, I will pay them fifty cents. I have over twenty-five dollars in my bank account saved from allowance, birthdays, and minor thefts. The collection in my closet grows. I'm swimming in Marilyns, but I don't know any more than I did before.

I still accompany my mother on her protest route. On the first delivery date for magazines for the week and for the month, she will drive from drugstore to drugstore and she marches in a tight little circle with a sign that I painted, which says IMMORALITY SOLD HERE. We don't go to the train station anymore. I like to watch her walk. She wears pumps, blue or white or red, which I think is an especially fine juxtaposition. She walks purposefully and gracefully, with a sort of catlike unselfconscious carefulness that can make no mistakes. Her heavily starched skirts sway with a vengeance. Her face is serene and righteous. If I could just figure out what really moves her, I think that I could learn a lot. A small crowd will gather and some of them will eye me either to judge how to respond to her or whether to pity me. I'm proud to smile at them as calmly as my mother and to watch that they are flustered by this impassiveness. A few of the women that I recognize from our street talk to my mother and she loses her calm when she discusses Marilyn. It is usually at this point that the shopkeepers come out of the store and try to add their two cents, or move my mother along. The men cannot budge her, but I notice that she is not adding substantially to her ranks either and none of the shopkeepers have given in to her demands to remove the offending magazines from their shelves.

Mother calls the PTA for an emergency meeting. This has never happened in summer before. One of my neighborhood informants, delivering his third Marilyn Monroe photo, says that his mother's bridge club could not finish their game because they got so wrapped up in discussing my mother.

"Is she crazy?" he asks. By punching him, I've lost a business associate and bloodied my hand, but it's worth it to get an idea of how I feel. Which is that she's not crazy even though she's certainly not right. Does that count as a feeling?

* * *

I dream that Marilyn Monroe is my mother. I always think of her as both names. I always dream of her floating in a pool on a pink raft. She says to me, Lucy, dear, I would give you advice on men and marriage because I have had a lot, but on the other hand, what I have done with what I had and the relation between what I wanted and what I got was not exceptional. Instead, dear, I would say to you my fondest wish is that you would be like an ice cube in a glass of Scotch. She licks her lips as she says this. Then she says, Usually champagne is my drink, but very few people know of my fondness for a glass of scotch now and again. She drinks champagne in a fragile glass as we speak, but she points to a glass at the edge of the pool. I paddle over to watch the ice float serenely, as if untouched, and bathed in the relaxing gentleness of the Scotch. I sip from the cold glass and it tastes like burned soap. When I turn back Marilyn Monroe, my mother, is gone. When I look back to the glass, however, the ice cube has dissolved into nothingness and water sweat rolls down the glass.

My mother thinks the PTA address went well, but I'm not so sure. I heard people giggling and whispering as they left the meeting. My mother is triumphant though when seven women call her to agree that the country is in danger of going into moral decline. They meet at our house and decide to picket the drugstores one more time before raiding the delivery trucks or something more radical. This time, however, after Mr. Franklin tries to talk her into leaving, he tells her, you have left me with no choice. Less than a minute later, a police car pulls up. Officer Lake tells my mother that she needs a permit to gather here. She begins to quote the Constitution, but he just smiles at her. The ladies keep marching in their circle, with full skirts swaying like pendulums. "Mrs. Kramer, what does Mr. Kramer think about this?" My mother does not answer. My father's opinion of this topic, if he chose to express it, does not interest her. Officer Lake appeals to the other ladies to imagine what their husbands will have to say if they are arrested.

"But Officer Lake," says one lady who is beginning to sob, "we are doing this in the name of liberty and decency.

Doesn't that count for anything?" "Not if Mr. Franklin says it doesn't." He smiles at my mother. "Freedom of speech," he adds. Only two women remain when Officer Lake has begun to talk reputation, and good name and upstanding pillars. My mother nods curtly at the other woman and I realize they have actively decided to follow this through. I see Officer Lake put handcuffs on my mother, who stands her ground as firmly as you can in heels, and when she is loaded into the police car, she raises her cuffed hands and waves sprightly at me.

Officer Lake tells my father that the car was towed to the police parking lot. "We could have impounded it," he adds, then counsels my father not to pay her bail until she has sat for a while. He does not, but only because he cannot find the check-book. My mother writes all the bills. The phone rings often and after a number of conversations where he is very quiet or tells them to mind their own business, he tells me not to answer the phone. I have to stay home while he goes out to get her. The Marilyns inside the closet smile at me a kissy smile. They don't care that my mother was put in jail for trying to help her country the best she knew how. I suppose it wouldn't be fair to ask Marilyn for compassion in this matter. You just can't tell from that smile if she'd be a compassionate person. Of course, it's her work smile. At the same time, it isn't fair to ask mother to live in the same house with all these Marilyns, so I take them off the door, peeling off the tape, and hide the stack in my mother's wedding album, which she keeps in a box on the shelf in my closet.

I dream that my mother knocks Marilyn over the head with a can of room freshener.

"Spraying is not enough!" she says. President Kennedy's huddled in a church folding chair and my mother grabs him by the arm, "Get up. Be a man again and run this damn country. We need you." He shivers. "No, Mrs. Kramer, we need you."

She stalls. "Well, I really need to mop my floors. That's what my husband got me that nice house for."

"Come on," says the President, "I'll do that for you."

* * *

My father pours cereal for my mother, who wears a sort of wise face as she listens to Dinah Shore talking to Liberace. Dinah does not look like she has ever spent four hours in prison. I feel less innocent, too.

Dinah is interrupted for a news bulletin: Miss Marilyn Monroe was found dead at her apartment this morning. An autopsy is . . .

"Apartment," snorts my mother without thinking, "not even a homeowner."

"Evelyn," scolds my father.

With her spoon, my mother dunks all of her Cheerios under the milk in turn. "Well, I killed a woman."

"Evelyn, that's not so," says my father gently.

She shrugs. She looks slightly pleased with herself. "I wasn't always like this, was I?"

My father shakes his head.

"I wonder what I will do now," she says. He looks around the kitchen, and frowns, then he gets up and stands at the back screen door, looking outside. "I really don't know." She joins him and takes his hand. "Well," she says, "it took me a while this time. . . ."

"Mother, you'll find something."

She laughs nervously. She knows that may not be a good thing for all of us. My father begins to clear the table.

"I want to get this mess out of the way," he says. The real sixties are fast approaching.

# FROM Atomic Candy

Phyllis Burke

How Fearfully and Wonderfully She Was Made
by the Creator!
—Book of Psalms

. . . But Hollywood and Americans who live
everywhere else were and are also accountable
before God for the elevation and eventual
destruction of this woman.
—Christian Century

In a way we are all guilty. We built her up to the
skies, we loved her, but left her lonely and afraid
when she needed us most.
—Hedda Hopper

The poor girl . . . Like a white dove . . .
One that hunters throw up in the air and shoot
as a target.
—Djuna Barnes

. . . Sacrificial lamb destroyed on the altar
of capitalism.
—Pravda

It was late in the afternoon on Sunday, August 5, 1962, the sun was hot and declining, and the sky was a seamless blue in Boston. Mayor Joe Albion escorted Kate, Marilyn, Nellie Kelly, and Mrs. Finnegan toward the small green wooden dock to board the swan boats on the lagoon in Boston's Public Garden. The excursion had been planned before he learned that Marilyn Monroe had died the night before. Nellie Kelly and Flora Finnegan watched Joe carefully for any signs of going on tour.

Joe Albion's emotions ripped through him, but he had remained as silent as the hard earth in a hurricane. He stopped before the Victorian-style flower beds, and he thought of graves covered with bright flowers. Unable to conceal the tears that welled in his eyes, he put on his sunglasses, which horrified Kate Albion.

"Politicians do not put on sunglasses, unless they are military dictators in South American countries," she said quietly to her husband. Joe did not respond.

Nellie Kelly leaned toward Mrs. Finnegan and whispered, "Here we go. He's going to lose it."

Joe Albion would not lose it. Not this time. He was a dandy, but he was not weak. He hated weak men. When he was a child, he had lived for a short time in Whittier, California. He had beaten a whining boy in the schoolyard. The teachers turned their backs and pretended they didn't see, as the other boys cheered Joe Albion on. Puppies can whine, he believed. That's their job. But a whining boy is a disgrace to his country and must never be allowed to become president. Joe Albion had beaten the boy so badly that he frightened himself. No one had stopped him. They should have stopped him, but they had cheered, and Joe Albion had become excited. His fists had struck this boy like he was hitting a toy. He had been seduced by violence. Later that day, he was alone in his backyard, sitting on the green grass near the flower bed. He saw the boy's blood on his shirt and he vomited onto the flowers.

Joe Albion composed himself. He was the mayor of Boston. He had never again beaten anyone, but Miss Monroe's death, her helplessness, her victimization, her vulnerability had made her too beautiful for him to bear. He believed that Miss Monroe could have lived happily with the snake in the garden, but that she'd left with Adam out of compassion. Pathological compassion. His hands and thighs ached from tension and remorse. He felt part of the collective responsibility for her death. Looking up from the flower bed, he saw his wife's eyes. He drew strength from Kate. Kate Albion would never have vomited on the flowers, but she did motion to Joe to remove his sunglasses, which he did. They continued on to the dock.

It was the last ride of the day, and Kate wanted to get this ride over with as quickly as possible. To her the swan boats were the type of ride you take in a bad dream where someone is chasing you but you cannot seem to run fast enough to get away from them or slow enough to be caught.

Ten-year-old Marilyn Albion looked at the swan boats. She had never seen anything quite so lovely, but her pleasure was tempered by the fact that Miss Monroe had killed herself. Marilyn Albion did not understand suicide.

The swan boats had six wide wooden seats, each long enough to sit six people. The bottom of the boat was a bright Kool-Aid green, and a red stripe ran along its wooden edge. The man-sized white swan at the rear of the boat, its feathers full and wide, its red beak and black Oriental eyes pointing down toward its breast, concealed in its back the seat for the young man who would steer and power the boat through the lagoon by peddling, his head riding just above the swan's.

Joe, Marilyn, Kate, Nellie Kelly, and Mrs. Finnegan boarded the swan boat and sat along the first bench. As they took their seats at the front of the boat, Marilyn thought of the *Hesperus*.

"Mr. Mayor, it's a pleasure to have you aboard, sir," said the young man who would be powering the swan boat.

"It's a pleasure to be here," said the mayor. "What's your name, young man?"

"Freddie Finney, sir," replied the young man, as he went to his position on the swan's back.

"Well, Freddie Finney, let's board these people and sail," said the mayor.

"Fatty Finney's youngest brother's oldest son," murmured Nellie Kelly to Mrs. Finnegan, who was discreetly adjusting her breasts to the absolute fascination of a little black-haired boy who was seated behind her.

"They're everywhere," said Kate Albion. "Like cockroaches. And every one of them votes. I love that family."

Excited citizenry boarded the boat behind the Albions. This was certainly history. No one could remember it happening in a nonelection year. Boarding behind them was a rollicking Italian family who took up two benches; a stern Irishwoman who had a fear of water, and her young son, who was the Mrs. Finnegan fascinatee; and two young women wearing bright summer peasant blouses and carrying newspapers and large pink cotton-candy swirls.

The last to board was Frances Bright, a strangely quiet bleached blond in her late thirties. Her makeup was slightly heavy, and although it was a hot, windless afternoon, she protected her perfectly built beehive with a small, sheer blue kerchief. Joe Albion studied her for a moment and turned away, embarrassed at his interest in her, Miss Monroe's body barely cold in its crypt. But this woman seemed out of place to him, as if she usually traveled in dark places. She sat alone on the last bench at the back of the boat, her knees locked together, her purse gripped tightly in her hands on her lap. Her fingernails were long and highly polished a deep and dangerous jungle red, and her white summer dress was made of such a fine light material that it lifted up around her on the power of whisperings and her own breath. She stared dreamily into the water of the lagoon and absently fingered the gold letter *F* pinned to her white dress near her heart. She was strangely alone, not a woman you would expect to see without a man on a hot Sunday afternoon.

The long strands of the weeping willow trees surrounding the lagoon brushed the side of the swan boat as it began its slow hypnotic glide across the water, beneath the bridge, and around the small island, just as it had done for almost a hundred years, probably powered by one of the Finney family.

The Irishwoman's young son tried to stand up and press against Mrs. Finnegan, but his mother grabbed him and made him sit, the slightest rocking motion of the boat terrifying her.

This is the hanged man.
Fear death by drowning.

One of the young women in a peasant blouse opened the late edition of the newspaper she was carrying and read it to her friend, who was chomping slowly and deliberately on her pink cotton candy like a praying mantis eating the head of her partner after sex.

It was learned that medical authorities believed Miss Monroe had been in a depressed mood recently. She was unkempt and in need of a manicure and pedicure, indicating listlessness and a lack of interest in maintaining her usually glamorous appearance, the authorities added.

"Well, I guess she was depressed," said Kate Albion, quietly and sarcastically. "Whoever wrote that better not be planning on the Pulitzer."

Marilyn will be dressed in a plain green dress, of a light shade, which she obtained in Florence, Italy. There will be no jewelry. The solid bronze casket will be lined with champagne-colored velvet.

"Champagne-colored velvet. Can you believe it?" said one young woman to the other.

The words "solid bronze casket" stabbed Joe Albion's consciousness and caused him great pain. Kate, Marilyn, Aunt Nellie, and Mrs. Finnegan stared straight ahead into the pleasant lagoon, knowing that the death of Miss Monroe was a tragedy for Joe Albion.

Looking as beautiful in death as she did in life . . .

The swan boat stopped dead in the water.

"It says that here. Isn't that the killer," said one of the young women. "She's dead! A beautiful dead body?"

Each member of the Italian family made the sign of the cross, like a row of holy dominoes, tears flooding their eyes.

Unclad body of star found on bed near empty capsule bottle.

The Italian family rattled their rosary beads for Marilyn Monroe's soul.

Marilyn Monroe committed suicide.

"She was killed," said Joe Albion. "She'd never kill herself. We all killed her." He crossed his arms against his chest.

Nellie Kelly and Mrs. Finnegan rolled their eyes and looked to Kate. "She better reel him in before it's too late," said Nellie Kelly to Mrs. Finnegan.

Marilyn Albion was sickened to learn they had all killed Marilyn Monroe.

The swan boat began to rotate in a circle. The Irishwoman with a fear of drowning was nearly in a faint, and her young son took the opportunity to reach from behind Mrs. Finnegan to cup that too tempting breast in his hand. Mrs. Finnegan took the little fellow's hand and would not let go, no matter how intensely he squirmed and pulled. He went into a panic, fearing he would draw back a nub as the rosary beads clicked and jostled for God's attention.

Kate Albion looked at Joe Albion, who stared straight ahead, marinelike, no tears, no movement. She tried to find the cause of the swan boat twirling in a slow-motion Edgar Allan Poe whirlpool. Freddie Finney had his face in his hands, and his shoulders heaved around his neck to shelter his sobs.

"Do you know what an autopsy is like?" said the young lady to her friend, who had gnawed the cotton candy down to the paper bone.

No. Joe Albion and Freddie Finney did not know what an autopsy was like, but they were about to learn. They were about to hear all about it, as the weeping willows tossed their long strands toward the water: how the medical examiner takes a saw and carves, as discreetly as possible . . .

"How discreet can you be with a saw?" said Kate Albion, looking up to the heavens. She turned toward the swan seat and commanded, "Freddie Finney. Pull yourself together!"

". . . through the skull, takes out the brain, weighs it."

"Freddie Finney. Your city needs you," said Kate Albion.

". . . takes out the liver, weighs it . . ."

"The ghouls, the photographers tried anything to get a 'good shot' of the corpse," said Mrs. Finnegan.

"Freddie!" said Kate Albion.

Freddie dropped his hands, and looking as much like the ancient mariner as a young man can, he dutifully peddled the swan boat through the lagoon. Mrs. Finnegan let loose the little boy's hand from her snare. He sat very obediently beside his mother, whose whole morbid life was flashing before her eyes. If she survived the swan boats, she promised St. Jude, her son would be a Benedictine monk.

"Miss Monroe was as popular in death as she was in life. And there are many who now say, Thank God she's dead. In six months, it will be as if she'd never lived," said the young lady licking away the last of the cotton candy.

The swan boat pulled into the dock, the last ride of the day.

"Marilyn Monroe will just be another dead sex symbol in hell," said the Irishwoman, whose son began to leap up and down in protest.

Everyone unboarded the rocking boat except Freddie Finney, the bleached beehive blond with the floating white dress, and Mayor Joe Albion. The two young women took their newspapers with them. The articles about Miss Monroe's death would be good material for their scrapbooks.

Kate, Marilyn, Nellie Kelly, and Mrs. Finnegan looked at Joe Albion, who remained in his seat at the front of the boat. Without speaking a word, Freddie Finney steered the swan boat back out onto the lagoon, his two passengers silent at opposite ends of the boat. Frances Bright's white dress hovered slightly above her body.

As they circled the tiny island, Joe Albion whispered, "Marilyn Monroe, why did you go?"

Mrs. Finnegan, Nellie Kelly, and Kate Albion sat sipping sherry in the library. Marilyn Albion, now in her pajamas, sat near them, playing with her Barbie doll in evening dress, the tiny zipper open at the back down to Barbie's waist. Barbie hopped like a foot-bound geisha back and forth at Marilyn's crossed knees.

The windows were open and not a breeze moved the draperies.

"Well, Mrs. Finnegan, have you heard about the copycat deaths?" asked Nellie Kelly.

"What are you harping on?" said Mrs. Finnegan, sipping her sherry.

"Beautiful women are swallowing bottles of Nembutal. They are being found dead with telephones in their hands. Nude. They leave notes that claim they follow in the steps of Marilyn Monroe," said Nellie Kelly.

Barbie was now naked and undergoing autopsy at the hands of the make-believe coroner, Marilyn Albion.

"Her soul's not going to go without taking a lot of them with her. It's the nature of the beast," said Mrs. Finnegan.

Marilyn Albion weighed Barbie's imaginary body organs.

"What would you be saying?" demanded Nellie Kelly.

"Marilyn Monroe was not just some poor little naked girl with a telephone in her hand. Marilyn Monroe had power. And you can bet that her power's going to look for somewhere else to settle in," said Mrs. Finnegan.

"I see what you're saying. Like the Banshee, in a sense," said Nellie Kelly.

Barbie's head was now separated from her body, and Marilyn put her finger into its surprisingly hollow cavity.

"Everybody! Happy birthday!" said Marilyn Albion as the sherry glasses were refilled.

Barbie's hollow head was as disappointing to Marilyn as the chocolate Easter rabbit she had bitten into last spring, only to discover it was an empty shell.

"What I'm saying," said Mrs. Finnegan, "is that a suicide makes the soul heavy, like any kind of violent death, and it stays on the earth for a longer period of time until it can work out its problem and move on."

"Little pitchers have big ears," said Aunt Nellie Kelly, noting at last the horrific Barbie doll scenario on the library rug. Kate watched Marilyn in silence. Nothing about Marilyn surprised her. This was, after all, the child who smuggled a picture of Richard Nixon into her house.

Lightning flashed. "Count the seconds until the thunder, and you know how far away the storm is," said Marilyn Albion.

"Aren't you clever!" said Nellie Kelly.

"Now back to where Monroe's soul goes," said Mrs. Finnegan.

"She wasn't just another brain-damaged blond, you know," said Nellie Kelly.

"Did you see that one at the back of the swan boat?" said Kate Albion. "The one my husband's still floating around with?"

Marilyn Albion could not get Barbie's head off her finger, which had swollen inside the cavity.

The thunder rolled more deeply toward Boston.

Mrs. Finnegan looked up and held her left index finger by the side of her head. "The thunder talks."

"What's it say?" asked Marilyn Albion, wondering if the thunder could be saying something specifically about her.

"It says, 'Time for bed, Marilyn Albion, so I can tell you my secrets,' " said Nellie Kelly.

Kate Albion said, "Does he see her face when he sleeps with me?" And for the first time, Kate felt jealousy, because now that Monroe was dead, she was perfect and ageless, and it was impossible for Kate to compete. Kate had been counting on Monroe becoming old, fat, and alcoholic.

This was too personal for Mrs. Finnegan, who adjusted her breasts while Mrs. Kelly escorted Marilyn up the pale staircase to her bedroom.

Alone and safe in her room, Marilyn Albion listened to the thunder and counted the seconds between rolls. Marilyn Albion believed that Marilyn Monroe was in between the thunder and lightning, trying to find a safe place for her soul, so it would not have to race through the world looking for a home. Marilyn tugged at Barbie's head, but the more she tugged, the tighter it held. A huge lightning bolt cracked through the sky and Marilyn's bedroom was as bright as a stage set. The bolt was followed by a thunderburst of such proportions that the vibrations poured into every house below, rattling the windows, knives, and toasters. Marilyn Albion looked at Barbie's head and decided it would be a nice safe place to keep Marilyn Monroe's soul. Small hot tears spilled from her eyes onto the decapitated toy.

In silence the swan boat plied its way through the lagoon until the night sky was slashed with lightning.

As a damp gust circled the swan boat, Joe Albion demanded, "What have we given?"

The blond then stood at the edge of the boat, heavenly and awful, as Freddie Finney peddled and Joe Albion sang a sad and soft sort of "Taps" for the dead goddess:

> Goodnight, ladies,
> Farewell, gentlemen,
> So long, everyone,
> It's time for me to go.

The swan boat tipped in one violent rock as Frances Bright jumped into the water . . . she did not surface. Freddie Finney backpeddled and shouted, "Mr. Mayor!"

Joe Albion turned to see the woman facedown in the dark green water, her beehive still intact. He jumped into the water and lifted her in his arms from death. As he stood up, he saw that the water was only a few feet deep. All she would have had to do was stand up. Lucky for Joe, she didn't know.

"Are you all right?" asked Joe Albion.

"If you save me, really save me," said the bleached beehive blond.

Joe Albion lifted Frances Bright into the swan boat, and Freddie Finney helped to get her seated. "It's time to go ashore, Freddie," said Joe Albion, the life force surging through him, a hero at long last. It wasn't the PT-109, but it would do.

Freddie Finney returned to his perch on the swan's back and peddled into the gusting wind and rain to the dock.

"Who are you?" asked Joe Albion, and the blond replied, "Frances Bright."

"Miss Monroe once said something that truly moved me," said Joe Albion to Frances Bright. Freddie Finney listened.

"What was that?" asked Miss Bright.

" 'You're always running into people's unconscious.' "

"Is that bad?" asked Miss Bright.

Joe Albion placed his arm around her shoulders and smiled. He would be patient. He would explain the world to her. She would be safe, and he would be redeemed.

The swan boat docked. Freddie Finney tied the boat up and followed Joe Albion and Frances Bright across the Public Garden toward the Blue Lagoon.

The abandoned swan boats bobbed on the dark green water, gentling nestling each other as birds do in a storm.

So long, Miss Monroe.
Fame has had you.

Marilyn Monroe— Neon and Waltzes

Nanci Griffith

The sun will stop shinin'
Hearts will stop poundin'
The screen is so lonely tonight
The men are out prayin'
The women are sayin'
She died for the loss of her prime
She lived on DiMaggio time

Farewell you old tinsel city
With your waltz in the mornin'
and your neon at night
I've bathed in your loneliness
Drank of your wine
I lived on DiMaggio time

Hearts felled to paradise still rest in her eyes
She was no fading light

Hot nights in August
So Long to the Goddess
"America's fatherless child"
Immortal's forever
That Queen of the camera
The master of winkin' a smile
And leaving her shadow behind

Farewell you old tinsel city
With your waltz in the mornin'
and your neon at night
I've bathed in your loneliness
Drank of your wine
I lived on DiMaggio time

Farewell you old tinsel city
With your waltz in the mornin'
and your neon at night
I've bathed in your loneliness
Drank of your wine
I lived on DiMaggio time

You: Coma:
Marilyn Monroe

J. G. Ballard

THE ROBING OF THE BRIDE. At noon, when she woke, Tallis was sitting on the metal chair beside the bed, his shoulders pressed to the wall as if trying to place the greatest possible distance between himself and the sunlight waiting on the balcony like a trap. In the three days since their meeting at the beach planetarium he had done nothing but pace out the dimensions of the apartment, constructing some labyrinth from within. She sat up, aware of the absence of any sounds or movement in the apartment. He had brought with him an immense quiet. Through this glaciated silence the white walls of the apartment fixed arbitrary planes. She began to dress, aware of his eyes staring at her body.

FRAGMENTATION. For Tallis, this period in the apartment was a time of increasing fragmentation. A pointless vacation had led him by some kind of negative logic to the small resort on the sand bar. In his faded cotton suit he had sat for hours at the tables of the closed cafés, but already his memories of the beach had faded. The adjacent apartment block screened the high wall of the dunes. The young woman slept for most of the day and the apartment was silent, the white volumes of the rooms extending themselves around him. Above all, the whiteness of the walls obsessed him.

THE ''SOFT'' DEATH OF MARILYN MONROE. Standing in front of him as she dressed, Karen Novotny's body seemed as smooth and annealed as those frozen planes. Yet a displacement of time would drain away the soft interstices, leaving walls like scraped clinkers. He remembered Ernst's 'Robing': Marilyn's pitted skin, breasts of carved pumice, volcanic thighs, a face of ash. The widowed bride of Vesuvius.

INDEFINITE DIVISIBILITY. At the beginning, when they had met in the deserted planetarium among the dunes, he had seized on Karen Novotny's presence. All day he had been wandering among the sand hills, trying to escape the apartment houses which rose in the distance above the dissolving crests. The opposing slopes, inclined at all angles to the sun like an immense Hindu yantra, were marked with the muffled ciphers left by his sliding feet. On the concrete terrace outside the planetarium the young woman in the white dress watched him approach with maternal eyes.

ENNEPER'S SURFACE. Tallis was immediately struck by the unusual planes of her face, intersecting each other like the dunes around her. When she offered him a cigarette he involuntarily held her wrist, feeling the junction between the radius and ulna bones. He followed her across the dunes. The young woman was a geometric equation, the demonstration model of a landscape. Her breasts and buttocks illustrated Enneper's surface of negative constant curve, the differential coefficient of the pseudo-sphere.

FALSE SPACE AND TIME OF THE APARTMENT. These planes found their rectilinear equivalent in the apartment. The right angles between the walls and ceiling were footholds in a valid system of time, unlike the suffocating dome of the planetarium, expressing its infinity of symmetrical boredom. He watched Karen Novotny walk through the rooms, relating the movements of her thighs and hips to the architectonics of floor and ceiling. This cool-limbed young woman was a modulus; by multiplying her into the space and time of the apartment he would obtain a valid unit of existence.

SUITE MENTALE. Conversely, Karen Novotny found in Tallis a visible expression of her own mood of abstraction, that growing entropy which had begun to occupy her life in the deserted beach resort since the season's end. She had been conscious for some days of an increasing sense of disembodiment, as if her limbs and musculature merely established the residential context of her body. She cooked for Tallis, and washed his suit. Over the ironing board she watched his tall figure interlocking with the dimensions and angles of the apartment. Later, the sexual act between them was a dual communion between themselves and the continuum of time and space which they occupied.

THE DEAD PLANETARIUM. Under a bland, equinoctial sky, the morning light lay evenly over the white concrete outside the entrance to the planetarium. Nearby the hollow basins of cracked mud were inversions of the damaged dome of the planetarium, and of the eroded breasts of Marilyn Monroe. Almost hidden by the dunes, the distant apartment blocks showed no signs of activity. Tallis waited in the deserted café terrace beside the entrance, scraping with a burnt-out match at the gull droppings that had fallen through the tattered awning onto the green metal tables. He stood up when the helicopter appeared in the sky.

A SILENT TABLEAU. Soundlessly the Sikorsky circled the dunes, its fans driving the fine sand down the slopes. It landed in a shallow basin fifty yards from the planetarium. Tallis went forward. Dr. Nathan stepped from the aircraft, finding his feet uncertainly in the sand. The two men shook hands. After a pause, during which he scrutinized Tallis closely, the psychiatrist began to speak. His mouth worked silently, eyes fixed on Tallis. He stopped and then began again with an effort, lips and jaw moving in exaggerated spasms as if he were trying to extricate some gum-like residue from his teeth. After several intervals, when he had failed to make a single audible sound, he turned and went back to the helicopter. Without any noise it took off into the sky.

APPEARANCE OF COMA. She was waiting for him at the café terrace. As he took his seat she remarked, "Do you lip-read? I won't ask what he was saying." Tallis leaned back, hands in the pockets of his freshly pressed suit. "He accepts now that I'm quite sane—at least, as far as that term goes; these days its limits seem to be narrowing. The problem is one of geometry, what these slopes and planes mean." He glanced at Coma's broad-cheeked face. More and more she resembled the dead film star. What code would fit both this face and body and Karen Novotny's apartment?

DUNE ARABESQUE. Later, walking across the dunes, he saw the figure of the dancer. Her muscular body, clad in white tights and sweater that made her almost invisible against the sloping sand, moved like a wraith up and down the crests. She lived in the apartment facing Karen Novotny's, and would come out each day to practice among the dunes. Tallis sat down on the roof of a car buried in the sand. He watched her dance, a random cipher drawing its signature across the time-slopes of this dissolving yantra, a symbol in a transcendental geometry.

IMPRESSIONS OF AFRICA. A low shoreline; air glazed like amber; derricks and jetties above brown water; the silver geometry of a petrochemical complex, a Vorticist assemblage of cylinders and cubes superimposed upon the distant plateau of mountains; a single Horton sphere—enigmatic balloon tethered to the fused sand by its steel cradles; the unique clarity of the African light; fluted tablelands and jigsaw bastions; the limitless neural geometry of the landscape.

THE PERSISTENCE OF THE BEACH. The white flanks of the dunes reminded him of the endless promenades of Karen Novotny's body—diorama of flesh and hillock; the broad avenues of the thighs, piazzas of pelvis and abdomen, the closed arcades of the womb. This terracing of Karen's body in the landscape of the beach in some way diminished the identity of the young woman asleep in her apartment. He walked among the displaced contours of her pectoral girdle. What time could be read off the slopes and inclines of this inorganic musculature, the drifting planes of its face?

THE ASSUMPTION OF THE SAND DUNE. This Venus of the dunes, virgin of the time-slopes, rose above Tallis into the meridian sky. The porous sand, reminiscent of the eroded walls of the apartment, and of the dead film star with her breasts of carved pumice and thighs of ash, diffused along its crests into the wind.

THE APARTMENT: REAL SPACE AND TIME. The white rectilinear walls, Tallis realized, were aspects of that virgin of the sand dunes whose assumption he had witnessed. The apartment was a box clock, a cubicular extrapolation of the facial planes of the yantra, the cheekbones of Marilyn Monroe. The annealed walls froze all the rigid grief of the actress. He had come to this apartment in order to solve her suicide.

MURDER. Tallis stood behind the door of the lounge, shielded from the sunlight on the balcony, and considered the white cube of the room. At intervals Karen Novotny moved across it, carrying out a sequence of apparently random acts. Already she was confusing the perspectives of the room, transforming it into a dislocated clock. She noticed Tallis behind the door and walked towards him. Tallis waited for her to leave. Her figure interrupted the junction between the walls in the corner on his right. After a few seconds her presence became an unbearable intrusion into the time geometry of the room.

EPIPHANY OF THIS DEATH. Undisturbed, the walls of the apartment contained the serene face of the film star, the assuaged time of the dunes.

DEPARTURE. When Coma called at the apartment Tallis rose from his chair by Karen Novotny's body. "Are you ready?" she asked. Tallis began to lower the blinds over the windows. "I'll close these—no one may come here for a year."

Coma paced around the lounge. "I saw the helicopter this morning—it didn't land." Tallis disconnected the telephone behind the white leather desk. "Perhaps Dr. Nathan has given up." Coma sat down beside Karen Novotny's body. She glanced at Tallis, who pointed to the corner. "She was standing in the angle between the walls."

A Dream Can Make A Difference

Beth Meacham

"And so, on this tragic thirtieth day of March, 1981, we look back at the life and death of a President of the United States, gunned down in the streets of Washington DC. To recap for those of you just joining us: This morning as the President was leaving a breakfast meeting, a man named John Hinkley, Jr., rushed out of the crowd, and fired three shots. One of those bullets struck home in the lovely curves of—"

"Cut! Cut, damn it! Dan, you can't talk about the President of the United States' tits. Especially when she's dead."

The anchorman stumbled to a halt. He wasn't used to doing standups outside the White House anymore, and the rain had rattled him. He glared at me, and I glared right back, waiting for him to realize that I was right. He did, too. I've worked with worse.

"Sorry. I just can't quite believe she's gone." Like nearly every man in the country, Dan was in love with President Monroe. She always did have that effect on men.

"Take a break." I turned to the rest of the crew. "Hey, ten minutes. Jim, go see if you can get some coffee. We've got half an hour to air, and I bet we get it in the can next time around."

I walked around our truck, through the maze of cables, and over to NBC's crew. They had Brinkley out in the rain, but he was hitting his marks just fine. He's an old pro, all right. I remembered watching him do the same thing right after the Kennedy assassination.

"Come to check out the competition, Linda?" That was Jane Mason, one of the best producers I know, except for me, of course. I just shook my head at her—we're old friends.

"Nope. Just getting away from the boys. I'm getting damn tired of fighting about the film clips; I don't know how many times this afternoon some jerk has had the bright idea to run that skirts-flying-in-the-wind shot against a sunset. Makes me want to puke."

Jane was sympathetic. She'd heard that one, too. "But Linda, you can't get too upset about that. She always did use sex appeal to distract them from what she was really doing."

"It's true. Man, I can't believe she's gone. It's like JFK all over again."

"Do you remember during the '76 primaries, when Buchannan came crawling in with that poll?"

"You mean when the Republicans had decided to accuse her of being JFK's mistress, and then Ford's people found out that if they did, she'd win for sure?"

"Yeah. Scandal from the past. They thought they had her. I wish I'd been there when those bastards realized that they were about to give the election to the Democrats." Jane seemed even more upset than I was. More angry.

Someday, maybe someday soon, I was going to have to write my memoirs of the Monroe years. I'd start when I stopped wanting to cry about it. Meanwhile, Danny-boy had had a long enough break. It was time to get this standup in the can. I wished to God that the White House would put out a new statement, so we wouldn't have to keep saying the same thing over and over. But Vice President Carter—no, President Carter—was still en route back from Central America, so there wasn't much to say. Hinkley was still being booked at the local precinct jail.

I first became aware of Monroe when I was in high school, because the boy I had a crush on only had eyes for her. It's funny. I don't remember his name, but I remember stuffing Kleenex in my bra and sneaking red lipstick to try to look more like her. That was in 1964, I guess, when she was making her comeback after the divorces, the suicide attempts, the

Kennedy assassination. She had a lot of guts, I realize now. Back then, I hated her. And I wanted to be just like her.

Three years later I was a freshman at UC Berkeley, and she was running for governor of California. Everybody laughed about it—Hollywood was creating real-life politics, with the sex goddess of the century in the leading role, and Ronald Reagan co-starring as her opponent. We all said that script-logic called for the two of them to run off and get married after the election, just like a second-rate Tracy-Hepburn film. But Reagan was fronting for the right-wing loonies who wanted to keep us in Vietnam, and Monroe was the Democrat's secret weapon candidate. And they were old enemies. I found out later that Marilyn blamed Reagan for Arthur Miller being called up in front of the McCarthy hearings, and had hated him since way back when. She told me once, in an off-the-record conversation, that the thing that finally made her agree to run was the thought of shoving it to Reagan. Of course, the fact that Bobby Kennedy himself had come to beg her to do it didn't hurt either. Oh, that woman had finally learned to make men jump through hoops.

That campaign was the dirtiest anyone's ever seen, before or since. Reagan's handlers dredged up all the stories about Monroe's affairs, and abortions, and drug addiction. They began to realize that they were making a mistake when the nude pictures turned up all over the country on people's walls. They knew they'd made a big mistake when Monroe went on TV and talked about how the studio doctors had forced her into the drug addiction to keep her skinny and passive, just like they did Garland and Taylor. I don't think I'll ever forget her performance that day, sitting there talking to Billy Graham, tears streaming down her face, about how in the dark of one August night she hit rock bottom and found God there waiting for her.

I guess nobody knows what really happened that night, but it was the last time Marilyn Monroe was ever known to have taken drugs. She left the U.S. and went into a sanitarium in Europe—the studio was furious that she wouldn't come back and finish *Something's Got To Give*, even though they'd fired her from it two weeks before. I heard rumors years later that the Kennedys had something to do with it, but by then her political links to Bobby and Teddy were so strong that nobody paid any attention.

She won the election. I had been working on her campaign, and was at the Monroe headquarters election night as a reporter from the Free Press. She walked right past me to get up to the stage to give her acceptance speech, and I saw her turn on the men who were escorting her. They'd been holding her arms on each side as if they were taking a prisoner to execution. She stopped in front of me, and jerked her arms away from them. She suddenly looked like she was ten feet tall, and she stared at all of them, one by one, and said, "I'm the Governor of California, not some doped-up party girl. Keep your hands off me from now on." She was whispering, like she always did, but it wasn't sexy.

Then she went up there and made a hell of a speech, all about how California was the richest state in the country, rich in money, but also rich in resources and people. She was going to make sure that those resources were invested for the future, by investing in people, all the people.

We got the White House standup done, and about half an hour later the rain finally let up. I had to get back to the newsroom; the network was starting to get pissed about my decision to tape the show on location—my job these days is producer of the Evening News. It isn't glamorous on the surface—hell, I'm not glamorous on the surface—but a lot of people depend on me to be there in the studio in case anything goes wrong. Nobody could understand why I assigned myself to this. I didn't understand it myself just then. I just knew I had to be there. Jane Mason understood. She was far too senior to be out in the rain producing standups. In fact, as I checked out who was on location at the White House this afternoon, I noticed a lot of senior women who shouldn't have been there—newswomen I first met on the Monroe campaign trails.

I got a call, then, that that bastard Hinkley was going to be transferred from the local precinct jail to the Federal Courts Building. I told Dan to stay at the White House in case there was any word from the vice-president. Then I called a backup crew and said I'd meet them at the Courts.

* * *

I saw her again a year later, in '68, at the Democratic National convention in Chicago. Martin Luther King and Bobby Kennedy had been assassinated, and the convention was in turmoil. She was there as head of the California delegation, of course, and she was tight with the civil rights people. I was out in the streets with the demonstrators against the war, real close to the hotel she was staying in. She walked out of the hotel into the middle of a riot, with a lot of TV cameras. There were always cameras following Governor Monroe. Some of the cops tried to make her go back inside, and some of the other cops tried to smash the TV cameras. They didn't want film of them beating up the demonstrators. But Monroe just walked out into the middle of the crowd and stood there in front of the cameras. A cop in riot gear came at her, and she batted her eyes at him and said that the last time anyone had swung a club at her it had been in Selma, Alabama. Everything calmed down real fast. Then she went to the convention hall, marched onto the stage and grabbed the microphone away from Daley. "Do you know that out there in the streets the Chicago police are beating up children?" she asked, breathy and trembling and aghast. Daley tried to shut her up, but couldn't bring himself to attack her physically for the mike. She talked for a long time about how the people outside were the children of the people inside, and how the convention should listen to them instead of punishing them for speaking out. She was electrifying.

Of course, the election went to Nixon in the end, but Monroe had become a national political figure. People started talking about 1972.

By '71 I was working for a San Francisco TV station, and I was assigned to cover the Governor. That was a pretty strange time. All the top political correspondents were men in those days, believe it or not. But after Monroe had read Friedan's book, she made a rule that she'd only do a press conference when there were at least ten women reporters in the room. And she kept giving exclusives to women, because she liked to talk in the ladies room during official functions. So all the papers and TV stations were scrounging around for females to send to Sacramento. We didn't get much air time; when

Monroe was talking to the men she'd turn on the high-voltage charm, and that was what the bosses wanted to show. But when it came to reporting the real news, they had to get it from us.

One night she found me sitting and crying in the ladies' lounge of the Beverly Hills Hotel. I was covering a speech she was making to the ACLU, or at least I had thought I was. The bastard of a news director had just told me on the phone that he was pulling me off the assignment because I had refused his advances two days ago. I wasn't cooperative, he said, and he only worked with *cooperative* women. Well, it got to me. Sometimes it seemed it didn't matter how good you were—the men in charge could only think about sex when a woman stood in front of them. So I was hiding out and wondering if I was going to say yes the next time some man made sex the price of a job, and hating myself for even thinking about doing it.

She came up behind me and said, "What's the matter, Linda?" in a real gentle voice, and I started talking before I turned around and realized who it was. I was embarrassed, I hadn't even realized that she knew my name. But I couldn't stay embarrassed for long, because she started imitating all the men who'd ever made her put out to get a job. God, she was a good actress. It was horrible, but in five minutes I was laughing so hard I'd forgotten that I'd been crying. Then she stopped, and said that she'd walked around for years just terrified of what she might be forced to do, until she realized that they *wanted* her to be afraid all the time. Because if they could terrorize her, they wouldn't have to admit she was as good as they were. "Honey, that man wants you to be in here crying, so you aren't out there competing with him. It stinks."

Then she pulled me to my feet, made my face up for me to hide the puffiness, and made me go out with her to the speaker's table. That was the first night she gave her famous sexual harassment speech. That was also the night I decided that she had to be President. See, she made that speech completely ad lib. She may have been planning to talk about women's rights, but she made all her points by linking them to the story I'd just told her, two minutes before.

* * *

100

I got to the Federal Building about 45 seconds before the other network crews did. A lot of people had gotten phone calls, it seemed. There was a message for me from Sauter saying that I'd better know what I was doing, because I'd missed the night assignments meeting. I knew that. We set up, and I grabbed a shirt and blazer from the wardrobe closet. I was going to have to go in front of the cameras for this one, and I wanted to look nice.

The Secret Service guys at the door said they didn't know a thing about moving Hinkley. Well, that's their job. But one of them had been with Monroe for years, since 1975, and he pulled me aside.

"Shut off that mike, Linda."

"Tim, I have to know where they're bringing him in— I need to see him. My viewers need to see him."

"Linda, shut it off," he repeated.

It was already off, of course. I showed him the switch.

He told me that the car was going to come in at the loading dock—I didn't even know the building had a loading dock. The only access was one alley, already blocked by blue-and-whites, so we couldn't get the truck in. I went and talked to the crew, and we decided I'd go with a transmitter and a camerawoman. As I strapped on the battery pack, I saw Jane talking with Tim. That man couldn't keep a secret, it seemed. Of course, Jane had been with us for years, too.

Monroe had a lot of support for the 1972 nomination, but not enough. I don't think she could have beaten Nixon, anyway; I don't think anyone could have. But after Watergate the country was disgusted with politics-as-usual. It was time for a change.

I had to make a tough choice at the end of 1975. I had two job offers—CBS News offered me a job as producer of their morning show. And Marilyn Monroe offered me a job as her media spokeswomen. I finally opted for the job with CBS, but it was hard. Monroe said she understood—I guess she did, too. During the campaign all that long year, she'd call me up in the middle of the night to talk about how things were going. She never once asked me to do her any favors, and I never once told my boss that she was doing it.

I did let her know what the press was thinking about, sometimes. Early on, during the primaries, people started wondering about men in her life. She was single, and had been for years. It hadn't bothered anyone in California, but they said that in Peoria people worried about single women. When I told her about that during one of our late night chats, she was pissed, but the campaign took steps to defuse the issue. I also warned her that stories about her and the Kennedys were starting to circulate again. She was actually happy about that one. She called it the Camelot Effect, and said it would win the election for her. She was right, too.

Whatever anybody might say now, in early 1976 nobody really believed that a woman could be elected President. The media followed her campaign for the nomination very closely, but that was mostly because she was so damned photogenic. The press attention kept her in the public eye, though. And people came to hear her speeches; after all, she was Marilyn Monroe and everyone knew her. They came to stare at her, but they couldn't help but listen to what she said. And what she said made a lot of sense. She talked a lot about the Constitution, and about civil rights, and about how we had a republic instead of a monarchy because individual people counted. She talked about her own past—there was a real Abe Lincoln-log cabin story—and explained why that meant she would be everybody's President, not just the bosses' President. People ate it up. They voted for her.

So she came into the 1976 convention with the nomination sewed up. The only question was who her running mate would be. I happened to be there, setting up for an interview, when she first met the Carters. The governor of Georgia had run a small campaign for the nomination, but he'd bowed out early when Monroe's strength became clear. He came to see her on the first day of the convention, and brought along Rosalyn and his mother, Miss Lillian. I expected fireworks—everybody knew that Lillian Carter was a rock-rib Southern Baptist. They talked for a while, and then Jimmy said straight out that he'd be honored if she'd consider him for her running mate. I think you could have knocked Monroe over with a whistle, she was so surprised.

"Jimmy," she said finally, "if you really mean it, we'd

win for sure. But they're gonna drag my morals all over the press. Can you handle that?"

Miss Lillian snorted. "Of course he can handle it. I've been watching you, Marilyn, and you're a good woman now, whatever you might have been once." Her sweet Southern drawl fell into a preacher's singsong. "I've told Jimmy, and I'll tell everyone else who asks, that if Jesus Christ could forgive Mary Magdalene, then Jimmy Carter can sure forgive Marilyn Monroe."

Marilyn looked angry at that. "I don't need your forgiveness for doing what I had to do to survive."

Miss Lillian nodded. "You bet you don't. But those good ole boys out there think you do. And if you get forgiven by the Southern Baptists, there's nobody going to dare bring up the subject again."

That old woman was sharp, and her son was a canny politician. And the combination of the Kennedys and the Southern Democrats was more than the Republicans could stand against.

I got into the Federal Courts building through the front door, then followed the crowd down into the basement. There were cops and Secret Service, and FBI, and about a dozen reporters and cameramen. Jane Mason was there, of course, but also Sue Leonard, and Barbara Short, and Sue Hardy, and a couple other women I recognized but didn't know. The five of us had spent a lot of time together covering Governor, and then President, Monroe. I wondered if they got late night phone calls, too. I wandered over to them.

"Hi. Guess we all had the same idea," I said.

"Guess so." That was Sue Hardy. There was a world of bitterness in her voice.

"Do you suppose we can get him to talk?" Jane asked.

That was what we were there for, obviously. If the Secret Service didn't want him to talk, we'd never have gotten this far. Tim was pretty transparent sometimes.

"Heads up!" someone shouted from down the corridor.

We turned like a pack of hounds and almost ran to the door. I slipped through the crowd toward the front, then turned and gave Janet, my camerawoman, a high sign and a sound check. She nodded. Jane bumped up beside me.

The doors swung back with a bang, and the corridor erupted in sound, cops shouting "Get back, get back!" and reporters shouting "Mr. Hinkley, Mr. Hinkley!" and "Commissioner!"

I took a breath, and stepped out right in front of Hinkley, so he had to stop. A hand in a blue sleeve reached for me, then was pulled back by another in a gray suit. I shoved the mike at his petulant mouth, and said, "Do you want to say anything to the American public?" Figuring, of course, that he must. They all did.

He blinked at me. Then he put on his TV face—everybody these days has a TV face—and said, "Yes, I do."

All the noise stopped, just like that. The Secret Service guys grinned. The cops looked sick.

"Can I say hi to my mom and dad?" he asked.

"Sure you can. Mr. Hinkley, why did you shoot the President?" I figured I might as well get to the point before somebody came to their senses and threw me out.

His face twisted. "She didn't love me," he said. I went cold inside. "She made me want her, and then she didn't love me." His voice rose. "She was a whore! She deserved to be punished, beaten. I could have made her listen, made her see that she shouldn't show herself like that, stand up in public like that. Women should take care of men and have babies, not spurn their love and make a public spectacle." He narrowed his eyes at me. "You're another one, aren't you. Another one of those half-women who like to make men small, like to see them crawl. Yes, I know who you are, you make men do everything for you, then you laugh at them and turn away—"

He went on like that. He was sweating, and the smell was nauseating. I wanted to throw up. The crowd was pulling back from him, but the cameras kept rolling, getting it all on tape. I felt a jab in my ribs, and turned toward Jane.

She had a gun in her left hand, the one by my side. She'd elbowed me, pulling it out of her pocket. I looked away quickly, and saw that Sue Hardy had one too. I was still holding the mike in Hinkley's face, so I jerked it a little to distract everyone's attention. That brought the cops back to themselves, and they grabbed tighter hold of him and got ready to move again.

That's when they shot him.

I remember lying awake late one night, thinking about all kinds of things. I'd just gotten off the phone with the President, who still called her old friends when she couldn't sleep at night. We'd talked about how well the Camp David meetings had gone, and what a good job Carter had done in making Sadat and Begin listen to reason. We'd talked about the new Job Corps program that she was going to propose, based on the California model that had been so successful. The economy was really taking off. I remember thinking how different everything would be if she hadn't run for governor, how close this country came to disaster during the Nixon years, when politicians really began to believe that the government was the master, and not the servant of the people.

Monroe brought compassion back to politics. She took that power she had, the power to make men want to please her, and turned their hearts toward kindness, made them want to heal the sick, and house the homeless, and teach the children, and not think of any reward but the knowledge of doing good.

She had told me about a dream she had once, that she was able to travel back in time to visit herself when she was fifteen. She'd open the door of her room, where she was lying on the bed crying and shaking. She'd walk in there, and take the pill bottle away, and tell the girl that if she'd just hold on she'd make a difference in the world some day. Then Marilyn said that in her dream she was flying from room to room, girl to girl, all over the country, and telling all of them to just hold on, they could all make a difference in the world, and then the world would be a better place.

Most of the men were satisfied with a smile from her. Most of them, but not that man who lay dead on the concrete at my feet. He thought that he could own her, like a dog or a slave. And he thought that he had the right to kill her if he chose, like a dog or a slave.

It was like the world had freeze-framed, or everything was in slow motion. I grabbed the gun out of Jane's hand, then someone grabbed it from me. The cops had dropped to the floor when they heard the shots, so they didn't see. The Secret Service guys deliberately turned their heads away. Both guns ended up on the floor at the back of the crowd, and when the FBI tried to pull prints, all they found was a blur of a hundred different ones.

I'm told that when the sequence was run on the news, Hinkley spewing hate and then the gunshots and his head exploding, people cheered. The thing I regret the most is that I wasn't able to cover her funeral. And without me there to stop it, Sauter ran the damn skirt shot.

They arrested us all, of course. They had to. After five days of questioning they let everyone but Jane and Sue and me go. But none of the video showed who had fired; and they couldn't tie the guns to any of us, because of the messed-up prints, and the fact that there weren't any serial numbers. The powder traces were on everyone who was close to Hinkley. And Tim was never called to testify. So the Grand Jury couldn't indict us, and we walked. Lost our jobs, of course. But we've formed a new media consulting company, Some Like It Hot, and we're doing better than ever.

I hope that Jimmy Carter can keep her dream alive into the 1980s. I think he's a better man than Lyndon Johnson was. I hope so.

Marilyn Sightings

Tom Whalen

1.

We entered MM's body at 0300. Penetration of the epidermal atmosphere had taken two hours thirty-three minutes due to the texture of the surface bubble and earthside error re the angle of entry. Sudden lightheadedness noted by several of the crew. Someone called out for his mother. Lt. Isserdorf said he had an urge to bake bread. "Loaves and loaves and loaves and loaves of fresh, hot bread." And indeed the cockpit was suffused with the smells of a bakery. The cabin lights flickered on and off before settling on a predawn glow.

2. FIELD REPORT: WITNESS #1

I knew Marilyn before the days of the reactors, before the time the raccoons suicided on her doorstep. Which made it even stranger when I saw her floating in a mayonnaise jar at Sam's Food Mart down the block. Surprised? Sure I was surprised. But there she was, about three and a half inches tall, her face poking against the glass. Had Sam bag the damn thing, took it home, but when I stuck my finger in the jar I couldn't find her. I emptied the whole jar on my Formica table, spread the mayonnaise with a wooden spoon, but she wasn't there anymore. What? Well, I felt kind of bad, you know, and for days I wanted to go out and commit grievous harm on the unsuspecting.

3.

Encephalic surges at 0333. Scent of gunpowder, of dead gulls. "My fingers feel funny," said Right Comdr. Whistle. I dreamed of bicycle spokes as we passed under the navel. Relays to the outside brought back sandwiches—tuna, ham, havarti. We drank wine and pondered the glazed ellipses floating outside the hull. Were they spectrum lines, sperm tails, traces? Inner convolutions? Pollen? Parchment scratches? Did it matter? Were we primarily researchers or cartographers? Biologists or geologists? We whirled around the zone of the navel for another hour tracking the strange ellipses that teased us again and again by promising messages then deferring them.

4. FIELD REPORT: WITNESS #2 (ROOMMATE)

We lived in a walk-up together for several months, before she dyed her hair or had met Joe or Art or Jack or any of those shits but long after Jim. My hair was already dyed, that's why I had so much trouble on the street. I had a taxi follow behind me when I went out to the drugstore for cigarettes or the deli for smoked salmon. Marilyn didn't like salmon. She preferred pig livers. What? Pig livers. I don't know how they taste, never ate them. But there she'd be, with her mousy hair and Minnie Mouse-y voice reading the dailies and slurping up pig livers. What? Fried. Broiled. I don't know how you cook them. What? A couple of months, like I said. I think she was—whatdoyoucallit?—dyslexic, that's it. When I asked for the salt, she'd pass the pepper.

5.

We glided through the endodermic planes beneath the limbs primordia, trusting neither our instruments nor instincts. Blue prominences flared up all around us. Right Rev. Boileau wanted to direct us to the lower region with its multitude of crossings, but we argued (in good faith?) that the files on this region were already too extensive. Forests of dendrite branches and ganglial cells as we maneuvered through the zone of rustling. And were those blackbirds we followed dreamed or real? Lt. R. Appleton looking up from her calculations said, "The actual path of an object may be complicated by the passing of another object, deflecting the gravitational attraction between the two. Such a deflection is called a gravitational encounter. But how am I to calculate the deflection if we ourselves are inside the object?"

6. FIELD REPORT:
WITNESS #3 (UNRELIABLE)

Sometime in the middle of the night she came to me, slipped noiselessly into my bed. I must have been asleep, because the first thing I remember is her sucking me, I thought I was dreaming, but the pleasure continued so I pulled back the sheets and saw the flash of blond hair bobbing up and down on my penis, but even then I didn't realize who it was. I knew it wasn't my wife, I didn't have a wife, or a girlfriend, at least not a current one, I was living, in a word, alone. Then she licked her way up my belly to my chest to my throat to my mouth then across my face where she tongued my ear, slobbered into it, which almost made me come right then, her tongue snailing in my ear, and then she whispered, breathily, the following: *I just love to read Wittgenstein, don't you?* And I knew then that somehow it was she, it really was *she*, reanimate, in all her perfumed glory, sliding my cock inside her.

7.

Behind the abdominal wall ran thickened strips, which we took as a road gelled with proteins and electrolytes. Honeycombed shells, ions sparking against the magma fibres. Permission for a fossil search refused. Gill shapes. Celluloid. Enameled air. Tracts of mother alveoli hypertrophied. "Metaphors, metaphors," Capt. Demeter said. "Metaphors and projections. What is it we wanted: perfection, motherhood, arousals bloody and bloodless? I am immune to marriage, to tiny birds in glass cages, to subsequent memories whose incestuous linkages strive against the will of the dripped furniture and eggshells of my days." Dr. Baubo shot him up with Demerol to ease his (our?) pain, and we rocked on, hoping we were making headway and not pathology.

8 . FIELD REPORT (VARIOUS)

Three sightings of large possibly female shape over I-10 between Houston and Austin. Shape did not move. Possibly cloud or reflection of sunlight off car roofs reforming on water crystals. Duration: 2 to 12 minutes./Simultaneous corpses: 4 female corpses fitting subject's description found in condo bathtubs in California, New York, Florida, Illinois. Bodies drained of blood. Eyes bluer than blue./Since '69 (first official records) annual average of eighty-nine stigmata sightings on the inner thighs of young women./On a beach reading *Jean Santeuil:* five witnesses./In a K & B Drugstore in Shreveport, La., slipping baby powder and Vaseline in a yellow purse: two witnesses (the manager and druggist)./Drownings: forty-seven./Entering UFOs: numerous. Narthexes, cathedrals, cars (foreign), cars (American) . . .

9 .

Nematoblasts and bronze flickerings condensing in the perceptual mist as we rose toward the large, cone-shaped muscular organ used for circulation of the blood. "A woman of this type directs the burning ray of her Eros upon a man whose life is stifled by maternal solicitude, and by doing so she arouses a moral conflict," said the blue parrot we kept in its cage throughout the expedition. "Jung?" I asked. "Squawk," it said. Surges of liquid gases, solar prominences and flares. How many associations are still undiscovered in our galaxies? Motion depends upon certain fundamental characteristics of a star cluster, but what motion was this we were experiencing as we sped toward the bright red organ? "I've got it, I've got it," Appleton said. "The kinetic energy of a star of mass m and speed v is $\frac{1}{2} mv^2$." We laid her out on the futon, wiped the sweat off her forehead, her upper lip, her arms.

10. FIELD REPORT: CREATION MYTH

There were seven dwarfs who lived in a dark forest and one day they came upon a tall fir tree (alt. version: hanging beech) whose limbs bowed down so invitingly that the seven decided they would rest here for the night. The first dwarf dreamed of a pool of clear water, though he had never seen a pool of clear water. The second dwarf dreamed of a smooth rock at the bottom of the pool, though he did not know what a rock was. The third dwarf dreamed of a fish swimming over the smooth rock at the bottom of the pool, though he had never before seen a fish. The fourth dwarf dreamed of light reflecting off the scales of the fish swimming over the smooth rock at the bottom of the pool, though he had no notion what fish scales were. The fifth dwarf dreamed of a moon that shone on the pool and the scales of the fish swimming over the smooth rock, though he had no earthly idea what a moon was. The sixth dwarf dreamed of a star-filled sky that held the moon that shone on the pool and the fish swimming over the smooth rock at the bottom of the pool, though he had never taken notice of the sky before. The seventh dwarf, who slept with his back against the fir tree, dreamed of nothingness (and of nothingness there is nothing to say). In the morning they came upon a pool of clear water in which a fish swam over a smooth rock, and beside the pool was a young girl whom they named Norma Jean and promised one day, if she obeyed them, to show her the way out of the dark forest and into a world of total light.

11.

Radiolarians and bivalves barnacled to the hull. Ganglia clogged our circuits. We were entering the higher functions where the limbic system (emotions, memories, sex, smell) bound gravity together like a knot in a firehose. Whatever could be demonstrated (compassion, hypocrisy, inflammation of the sex organs), was, as long as it remained nonverbal. A wheel, a drum, flatworms, rejuvenation, two individuals attempting by force to continue existence long past logic allowed. Neurons firing back and forth. Electric flowers. Our charts no more than confetti. Thalmic variations (chemicals cupped in a forgotten cavity) flooded the zone. I saw a mountain where no mountain should have been. I saw regicides and veins empty as early morning highways. In the amygdala I expected to find humor, but saw only the dim light of pathos. Helmholtz postulated that the source of the self's light was the conversion of its gravitational potential energy into radiant energy, but our computers couldn't agree. Captain Albert (or the ghost of Captain Albert) appeared to us and said, "Don't forget that the slightest deficiency in m can cause a mass defect of the nucleus beyond anyone's imagining," then he vanished back into the cortical pool. Capillaries as big as my thumbs. Dendrites tall as firs. Ellipsoidal plants dressed in elegant gloves dancing like angels on the hindbrain. Isserdorf screamed, Boileau had to be restrained, Walker took out his gun and looked at it wonderingly. Here, within the meninges, her depression around us as thick as sperm, we were adream and dumb as the day we were born.

12. FIELD REPORT: ASCENSION

. . . because when you're acting you're not you, the you is elsewhere, and for a while you forget you're you, you're whoever you're supposed to be playing, but then something happens, you know you're you, but you can't find this you, you can't find yourself, and the character you're playing knows this as well, and she begins to look for you, both of you begin to look for you, but you're not there, the other is you, but you are not the other, you want to be elsewhere, you want to be with you, but where is that, who is that? A wind, a song, a tablecloth, a subway grate—are we pulled out of ourselves by the objects, the sounds, the smells around us? Apotheosis not found in multiplication. Poetry not information. The unutterable within the uttered.—Wittgenstein. Walking to school, not walking to school: the looks take you away from yourself. Beginning, not beginning. Ending, not ending. Cinema: the hemorrhaging of images.

1 3 .

We sliced through the sclera and choroid layers and tacked through the vitreous humor for several hours, riding whenever we could a resurgent cone impulse. The cabin was quiet, except for the steady whimpering of Isserdorf, which no one commented on, or perhaps no one but I heard. A distant earthside light led us toward the ciliary body and from there south to the window membrane, and by 0300 the next morning we had exited Marilyn.

The Real
Marilyn Monroe

Hillary Johnson

It happened on a Sunday in 1975, when Marilyn Monroe ran out of Dom Pérignon on page three of her memoirs, shortly after sunrise. The maid was still in bed, and since Warren never slept over, she put her long brown hair in a ponytail, took off her makeup, and got in the Honda.

By noon she was somewhere in West Covina, Mantovani on the AM radio, still looking for a supermarket with a friendly aspect. Sometimes it's hard to make a decision.

And sometimes it's made for you. In Marilyn's case, this had happened so often that when she saw a yellow banner in a shopping mall parking lot, over a red-and-yellow-striped tent, proclaiming BARBRA STREISAND! DIANA ROSS! MARILYN MONROE! TODAY AT NOON! she pulled over at once and hastily applied lipstick.

At the stage door, a grumpy little man in a rumpled suit, who looked like Tom Ewell had looked after lunch breaks, eyed her up and down and growled, "No autographs!"

"No, no autographs," Marilyn sighed in relief.

The little man scowled. "What do you want, sister?"

Marilyn had left her date book in Beverly Hills, so she didn't know. "I'm Marilyn Monroe," she offered, feeling rather stupid.

The little man looked angrier than ever. "Well why didn't you say so! You're late, get in there! Gina! Marilyn's here!"

Marilyn flapped through the tent and was seized bodily

by a red-haired waif with a mouth full of safety pins. The girl tongued the pins to the corner of her lip and drawled, "Thumb on, thisth way."

In the dressing room, Gina spat the pins into a ceramic dish full of the same. Marilyn, being Marilyn, wondered briefly if these pins were the effluential by-product of some strange bodily malfunction or addiction, causing Gina to spit up metal on a regular basis and thus relegating her to a life behind the scenes. She liked Gina right away.

Gina flung a white halter dress with a full pleated skirt at Marilyn. "Wear this. Don't mind the coffee stains," she said. "Have you ever done this before?"

Marilyn looked around the crowded dressing room, racing with lithe young men and assorted stagehands. She and Gina were the only females. There seemed to be nowhere else to change. "Yes, of course," she said helpfully, not sure.

The dress fit perfectly. A young man in a cowboy getup told her so. "Git alawng, little dogie!" he said, in fact, tipping his hat.

"Over here," Gina said, plunking her down at a makeup table.

"Who was that?" Marilyn asked.

Gina made a face. "That's Rodeo Bob. He's the opening act. Rope tricks. Don't worry, he always says that."

Down the row of mirrors and lights, Marilyn saw Diana and Barbra. She smiled at them. They smiled back. Gina opened a makeup tray. "You need help, or do you do your own?"

Diana and Barbra looked so fabulous, so young, so much larger than life, that Marilyn's heart sank. "I need help," she said breathlessly. "Is there any champagne?"

Diana let out a screeching, raucous laugh. "Oooh, you're good, girl!" she said. "Hello, *Marilyn!*" Barbra called out in her best Brooklynese. "Where's your ukelele?"

Marilyn felt better, and relaxed while Gina did her face. The touch of a makeup artist had always filled her with longing, especially when the makeup artist was a woman. It was too much like having your diaper changed. Someone cracked her a beer.

"You're getting old to play Marilyn," Gina remarked

casually. "You might try doing Liz sometime. You have the tits for it."

Marilyn sat up. "But I *am* Marilyn!"

Diana rolled her eyes. "God!" she said. "Another method actor!"

Gina shrugged. "We'll just have to make do. You have good skin, but the hair I don't know about. Did you bring your own wig? Never mind, I've got one."

The beer helped. Marilyn stood in the wings, scratching under her wig, listening to Barbra and Diana belt out a duet of "Ain't No Mountain High Enough" to a chorus of lewd catcalls, whistles, and insinuating remarks.

By now Marilyn had begun to question this strange, unpublicized booking at a shopping mall in West Covina, but there seemed to be a kind of internal logic to it. She began to think that she was fated to be there, for there was no other explanation.

Barbra finished the set and strode offstage, flinging her wig off her bald head. "Bastards! I hope their fathers all fuck them in the ass!"

Diana followed. "I hope their fathers all fuck *me* in the ass!"

"You're on!" growled the nasty man in the rumpled suit, grabbing a microphone. "Ladies and gentlemen—Marilyn Monroe!"

Marilyn wobbled onto the boards. She could dimly see the red and yellow stripes of the tent through the cigarette smoke. A hard white spotlight was fixed center stage like a pillar of salt, and she dutifully inserted herself in its beam.

All of a sudden the silky dress rose up around her like a flight of angel wings, fluttering deliciously against her cheeks. The audience roared with lustful derision, an autonomic howl rising from every throat, while another voice inside her remarked coolly, "Norma Jean Baker, this is your life."

And it wasn't so bad. There in the alar cocoon of the white skirt she felt herself enveloped by a rare kind of privacy, an exotic flowering of solitude that she was loathe to interrupt. A small thing really, but for the first time the choice was there, and she let it wait for one purely selfish moment, a moment so slight that no one but she would ever know it had passed. And then, as always, but no longer inevitably, she became Marilyn.

The prettiest girl in the world kicked her legs out wide and leaned forward, squeezing her breasts together with her bare arms and reaching toward the hem of her skirt with elegantly splayed fingers.

"Oooh," she cooed, "isn't it delicious?"

And it was. She had always liked the feeling of wind between her legs, even more than she liked champagne. She decided right then and there not to write her memoirs, even if they made her give back the money. No sense looking back. Instead, she looked down. Rodeo Bob grinned up at her through a gap in the floorboards, holding a table fan set on high. He gave her a thumbs-up, and Marilyn gave him back the legendary wink. He was kind of cute. It was love at first sight, and it would last forever.

Sex Appeal

Rita Valencia

A woman poses at her mirror and begins to strip the clothing from her perfect body. She has the shape of an hourglass. A promising stranger might find her slightly severe. Her beauty does not know how to forgive. It bruises with a relentlessness that only her body can satisfy. Gazing into her own blue eyes, she practices repeating, "I am falling down a deep well."

After a moment's contemplation at her closet door she dresses for the evening's party: pushup bra, black silk stockings, high heeled pumps. In this condition, who would not want her? But as she arrives at the party she becomes conscious of a colic in the throat. She fetches a Scotch and finds an unoccupied corner in which to drink it. Her solitude is soon interrupted by a confident man.

His identity is not important, he is just an actor who enters the woman's crisis and exits after his opening line.

"Hi, my name is X. And who are you?"

She responds:

I am the dark disturbed shadow of Marilyn Monroe.

No one can see me, they only see her.

They want to walk in her shadow. That means fuck.

I pull this phrase out of thin air and force myself to live with it for a while. The statement is both true and untrue. The untrue is a cruel sister to the true. It insists that I am indeed myself, none other; that Marilyn Monroe was some woman who became a movie star but was too unbalanced to survive her troubles. It further comments that "dark disturbed shadow" cannot be a separate entity from Marilyn herself. Now, untrue's attitude is literal and unpoetic, and might miss a more subtle aspect of the statement, or perhaps a more obscure one, because on the face of it, the statement is rather

118

brash and unsubtle, but I won't entirely discard untrue's position because it is like a needle poised at the eye of the true, forcing her to be honest or else.

I am the dark disturbed shadow of Marilyn Monroe.

No one can see me, they only see her.

They want to walk in her shadow. That means fuck.

Slice into the poetry of that statement. It has rock 'n' roll quality. Remember "Walking the Dog?" Fucking the Bitch? I'm discussing charm. I'm saying that when a man looks at me he first sees Marilyn Monroe, because I am blond, blue-eyed, and possess an hourglass figure. What you see is beautiful and smooth. As your love pours down me and passes my throat I undulate. The light begins to fall away in curves. I become complex and irregular, full of crevices, folds and furious indentations. You complete me in an obscure passage of discordant song that echoes below a straight four beat. Hit it:

I am the dark, disturbed shadow of Marilyn Monroe.

No one can see me, they only see her.

They want to walk in her shadow. That means fuck.

Sex appeal is an implication. Freud, the master of logical observation, has said that mechanical concussion leads to sexual excitation. In the case of injury, libidinous energy flows to the affected area in order to blind the trauma. Sex appeal draws to its possessor innumerable psychic concussions. The impact of a glance full of desire, the implication of severe sexual aggression, suffuses me with libidinous energy. I become Marilyn Monroe. I become a sealed system. Internally there is distress. My throat tightens, I am all choked up, but I can't stop the flow of my disintegration. I am not Marilyn Monroe. I am the dark disturbed shadow of Marilyn Monroe. I possess an hourglass figure. You turn me upside down.

Marilyn Monroe is beautiful. She possesses an hourglass figure. Think of her as an hourglass just turned on end, in whom the sand is pouring down. The hour is passing. She is in distress. She doesn't think of why. She is trying to add more sand. It is not that she wishes to add more time to the hour, it is that she is determined to fill the vacancy it creates in its passing.

"Oops," says Marilyn. "I seem to have lost my—uh—something!"

Nobody can say oops like Marilyn. Nobody can render distress with such charm. It is part of her unique sex appeal.

I am the disturbance in the shadow of Marilyn Monroe. I am the flowing of the sand. You set me in motion when you look at me as if you want something and I know what. When you look at me like that, I cannot help but recede, holding before me the panty shield of Marilyn Monroe, on which her image is reproduced five thousand times in colored silk-screen. Let that multiplicity of woman equal my libidinous shield. I am a disturbance that exists in obscurity. I connive, contrive, I twist on the knife you thrust through the curtain. Then, when you feel you have me skewered, I skew, slip away, cast a dark look into your eyes; and you believe I must be a mystery after all.

There was once an old woman who put her hand in a velvet puppet. She herself had been a great beauty, a star of the silver screen. Her career ended hardly a decade after it began, but she retained her good cheekbones. Now she lived in a modest apartment across the courtyard from the young Marilyn. Marilyn came to her one day, very excited. A friend had arranged an interview with one of the most powerful agents in Hollywood. Marilyn asked the old woman what she should wear, to which she queried:

"How much money do you possess?"

"Five hundred dollars," replied Marilyn.

"Give it to me," said the old woman.

Now the old woman was no common thief. She had the power to multiply that paltry sum by infinity or more, and had no desire to hold even a hundredth of a percentage point back as a fee. Marilyn did not know this, however, and handed over the money because the old woman was always so disarmingly cryptic. "I am taking this so that your powerful agent will not," said she.

"The first thing you must do," she counseled Marilyn, "is to put the appointment off for at least a week. Speak to the agent personally. Since he has been so kind as to see you, you wish to be so kind as to personally explain the delay and not have it related through the secretary. Tell him you must fly to Des Moines, Iowa, for a week to pose for a farm tractor advertisement. Then say precisely these words: 'But I'd love to come see you as soon as I'm home again.' "

Of course, the old woman was a great magician and a sorceress. She knew that sex appeal resided in implications. The message she gave to Marilyn to repeat was resplendent with images of virtuous fecundity.

I am a disturbance that exists in obscurity. I pour into the bottom, the obscene buttock, the dark one. Spank me, turn me upside down, and I drain. Once upon a time I wrote poetry. The subject was a secret love affair, from which I suffered repeated mechanical concussions. I was in school at the time, and married. The poems were well received by my teachers, all famous and well-published poets, but I knew these poems were shit. All I really wanted to say was, "I want to fuck you, McConnell, I want to fuck you till the cum pours out of my ears. I don't care what it destroys. I don't care if my husband goes off and kills himself, if my father drops dead of a heart attack, my mother jumps off a bridge, I just want to go on forever with you inside me fucking and sucking until we melt in the heat of our own hell," etc. And where was the poetry in this? It was in the seamless, soothing, wistful words of concealed obscenity. The face of Marilyn Monroe, my double. The smooth glasslike surface, the hourglass figure, through which pours the sand, the ground fragments, the crushed stone, the suffering concussions of multiple appraising glances that say, "Give me time. I know you want it. My clock is running."

The old sorceress, magical first lady of the silver screen who lived now in obscurity, had been waiting for an opportunity to apply what she had learned of sex appeal to an appropriate subject. Long ago she had sustained a bizarre injury that left a sewing needle embedded in one of her eyes. It put a premature end to her career, but she was able to bear up, through sound financial planning and a sturdy cynicism. She hired an unemployed set builder to create a special room for Marilyn to inhabit until it was time for her appointment with the powerful agent. (Hollywood is full of secret places where metaphysic rituals transform simple loveliness into devastating glamour. This chamber was not the first of its kind.) A little bed dressed in pink stood in the center, a gorgeous Chinese carpet of thick pile covered the polished marble floor. The lighting was soft and there was music: Count Basie, Duke Ellington, Tommy Dorsey. The old woman set out one of her prized garments for Marilyn to wear: a negligee of imported silk in shell pink with ecru lace.

On the walls hung one hundred photographs of Marilyn Monroe, public and private, nude and clothed, photographs that would become legends around the world. The centerpiece of the gallery was a full-length mirror in a handcarved wooden frame. The old woman positioned the mirror so that the light falling on Marilyn's face when she looked into it would be more flattering than in any other place in the room. Thus, if all she wanted to know was how pretty she was, she could rest completely assured.

The sexually appealing image is the sealed-off image. Marilyn Monroe is to be completely immured in the ideal of her beauty. I am what flows downward through the hourglass. My wasplike waistline conceals an infantile colic which matured to nausea and proceeds to metastasize through the system.

Imagine yourself traveling downward in an elevator. Its shaft is infinitely long. Once you have learned to gracefully accept eternal falling, you must become used to the sensation of the sand slipping perpetually over the smooth inner surface. No matter how you choke up, the spasm is always illusory, for the diameter of that passageway is not subject to fluctuation. It does no good to feel sorry about this constant downward disintegration, one can indulge in the temporary narcotic of denial, of changing identity, but it is impossible to forestall that moment of quiet wakefulness in which sex appeal reveals itself as a calamity of obscure origin, a steel needle in the flesh eye. It becomes obscenity: the cruelty that exposes itself only in the whisper of malicious secrets; the connivance of an envious old woman. And the old woman is aware that sex appeal is the hour that seems never to end; she is also aware that none of the photographs in the underground chamber show Marilyn growing elegantly aged, just a sadder and more complex thirty-five.

* * *

Marilyn was not ordinary. The old woman had sensed this fact, but when Marilyn walked into her shrine, her sense was confirmed. At Marilyn's first glance, she responded with the remark, "So it's really true." Then Marilyn strolled through the room smiling. Her smile was a peculiar mixture of a lost queen reinstated upon an all-new throne and a poor country girl who has just been shown the palace she will inhabit forever after.

The normal woman will react with some suspicion when presented with a palace. The queen will immediately ask herself, "And whom must I behead to protect my new position against envy?" The poor country girl will immediately ask herself, "Will there be no less a price than my very soul, or worse, that of my mother's, for such splendor?" But Marilyn's queen was eager to throw her first ball, and her country girl was all innocent avarice. It could not have been more obvious to her that the old lady had been dabbling in the dark crafts, but Marilyn, being the unique and suggestible person she is said to have been, would be just the type to walk into her trap all wide-eyed and then say "oops" once the door slammed shut.

The old woman was puzzled. Although she knew that a part of Marilyn was ready to bond with the filmy divine garment of glamour, she had expected that such a display would, on first glance, frighten poor Marilyn. The old woman had a speech made ready for this situation, a speech that would go something like this: "You must believe in magic just as you believe in gravity." The speech was unnecessary. This girl was too quick to need it. As a matter of fact, she seemed to require quite the reverse of such advice, and so the woman said: "My dear, you must believe in gravity just as you believe in magic."

Marilyn laughs like the gay bursting of a crystal goblet on a marble floor.

The normal woman will react with some suspicion when presented with a phallus. Down below there is a woman who does not suspect the phallus. With a sense of eagerness and goodwill she takes off her blue jeans, slipping her panties over tender and voluptuous buttocks. She unfastens her little white brassiere, transforming the exquisite volumes of her breasts from the cone shape of the 1950s to soft and merciful spheres. She puts on the pink negligee and drifts happily around the room, as if telling all those other Marilyns, with the glee of an eighteen-year-old: "Here I am, the *real* me!" The ingenue pulls the fabric of her gown tautly across the surface of her thigh. She is learning: she is comparing the silk to the creamy skin of her inner thigh. She is comparing the downy hair at the nape of her neck to the frothy golden abundance of her pubis; the slick ivory surface of her teeth to the slippery smoothness of her pussy; the dimunitive pucker of her lips moist and ready for a midnight kiss to the curious nether pucker of her virginal anus.

She wishes to learn more. She gazes at her seamless beauty in the looking glass. She learns the curve of her jaw is an effortless line. I wait. I am the tortured scrawl of foresight. Her cheeks are flushed with anticipation. Her eyes are delicately shaded with the darkness of annihilation. They look searchingly into the eyes of the beholder, saying, *save me, I am falling down a deep well*. She has slipped onto the smooth glasslike surface, where her image is camera-ready and may be reproduced easily in the imagination as an abstract shape of perfect symmetry. I wait. I am ground into sand.

The old woman sits at her kitchen table staring into her Scotch. The ice cubes clasp within their molten forms the phantasms of her remorse: small human figures twisting upward, heads screwed entirely around, regurgitating fire onto their own backsides in a Christian inferno. All her life she has been moving towards moments like these, of utter immobility, where even the movement before her eyes is locked in ice. What a trivial lie: those sweet moments, when her every command is obeyed, when the diabolical shrine is under construction, the portraits positioned just so . . . "Here, Madame?" "No, over there, ahh, just right, Mmm. Now move it a little to the left." "Oh, Madame—what a stroke of genius to position it just so." At the kitchen table, staring into a tumbler of Scotch, she becomes tormented with the notion that her power is false and stupid. The shrine, the design, is not wizardry, but the work of a petty old busybody with a needle stuck permanently in her eye. In their ultimate garbling, magic and gravity come to the same end. The girl, the poor little one, the stupid queen whose grandiose self-deceit would pump her into the capillaries of ten million testicles—she would amount to nothing more than crumpled paper.

At her advanced age, the perfect bitterness of the old woman's reflections is more satisfying than those mendaciously gay moments when she plays the clever old sorceress. But the old woman is not to be allowed the full articulation of her despair, for there is a sound outside. With her wise landlady's ear she detects a burgling. She rises from her table and fetches her cane.

The disturbance comes from Marilyn's apartment. She listens at the door, looks through the window and sees a light go on, deeper in the house. Stealthily the old woman makes her way through the flower beds to the rear of Marilyn's bungalow, where she peers through the bedroom window. The man is very young, slender as a whip, with dark hair and pale skin. He sits on Marilyn's bed, moving his hands over the covers rhythmically, his gaze falling on her pillow, her dressing table, the open drawer in the bottom of her wardrobe, from which something silky drapes.

The old woman is waiting for the young man to move so that his shoes are visible to her. If they are not the right sort of shoes, she will call the police. The man stands up and walks to the wardrobe, where he pulls the undergarment, a silk teddy, from its drawer. Holding it to his face, he unbuttons his shirt, unfastens his belt, unzips his trousers. All this the old woman watches with great patience and equanimity. Still his feet remain hidden from view by Marilyn's bed. She can only see the tensing of the muscles in his buttocks, the quickening rhythm of his arm. The old woman has seen a great deal in her life. None of it amounts to anything. She simply waits at the window to be assured that his shoes are correct. The young man gathers the teddy around his erection and sits back down on the bed. He twists the garment into a cord and winds it around his penis, tightening it, loosening it. It takes a very long time for him to change position, but finally he gets down on his hands and knees upon the bed, with the teddy spread out beneath him, revealing his relatively new cordovan loafers and argyle socks. He passes; probably a poet or a law clerk.

This is the night time, where everything collapses in the dark. It is the narrow waist of the hourglass, the slenderest moment of all. When you look at me like that, I cannot help but fall, I crumble into grains so small that I trickle through the throat of the hourglass. Marilyn Monroe is in the shrine in the basement. Don't worry about her. I'm up here in this room, with this whip-like boy. I like him you see. He makes me feel invisible. He breaks down my logic into dumb lyrics, into a paperback romance. He inspires me to shave my underarms. I want to amuse this young intellectual. Let's play dictionary. I'll be the word, you guess what I mean. Fucking me is like fucking intelligence. With great equanimity and patience I obscure myself in the garden. I remove myself to the garden, where philosophers roam who want to fuck me with a bag over my head on which Marilyn's face is silk-screened. Hear me scream with orgiastic delight as he whispers such nothings in my ear as: "Nature has taken care of you: instinctively you see blindly with greater clarity than the most sharp sighted reflection on the male, instinctively you see where it is you are to admire, what it is you ought to devote yourself to." Bend over, I tell him. I'll pretend I'm a boy. Take off those stupid shoes, they make you look like a law clerk. Leave on the one sock. I have this instinctive feeling I should devote myself to you, whip-like boy, with you flashingly passionate logical eyes which simplify me into an abstract shape of perfect symmetry. But my devotion is not all I have to give you, whipping boy. Now that you have served as the auto-eroticist who comes to masturbate in Marilyn's empty house which she has abandoned to worship in the shrine of her self, I will reveal my condition to you.

I am the dark disturbed shadow of Marilyn Monroe.

No one can see me they only see her.

They want to walk in my shadow. That means fuck.

With my limpid blue eyes and wavy blond hair, my perfectly voluptuous hourglass figure, I can go anywhere in the world and on first glance, people will see me as Her sister, a goddess. As the dark disturbed shadow of Marilyn Monroe, I am not, as the poem implies, a separate entity from Marilyn. But I am not integrated either. Dear whipping boy, it is my misfortune to slip down your belly, to slip through the glass. If only I could heap blame on you, whipping boy. I cannot, however. I cannot hold you responsible for the suffering concussions, I cannot make you pay for the fact that when you look at me I crumble into grains so small that I trickle down through the throat of the hourglass.

I am the inarticulation. I am the stutterer, choking on the sharpness of my glasslike body. My seamless beauty is reflected in the looking glass, but a violent act shatters it into a thousand pieces. Mechanical concussion must be recognized as one of the sources of sexual excitation. Sex appeal consists of a crucial simultaneity: the beauty exists, both seamless and violently shattered, in the same place at the same moment.

The old woman, who has resumed her place at the kitchen table with a fresh tumbler of Scotch, stares into her ice cubes again and hallucinates Marilyn in her little shrine. Have the girl's thoughts grown morose down there? The young man in Marilyn's room is just the first of a million or more fans to come. The whole business of sex appeal proceeds just fine without the issue of mortality entering in.

She goes to Marilyn's apartment later and quietly pushes open the bedroom door. Marilyn has not returned, and the young man is gone. The old woman takes the dirty teddy from Marilyn's bed and smooths the bedcovers. Returning to her own apartment, she runs the sink full of warm water and leaves the garment to soak.

Morning. Sunday. Marilyn has still not returned. "I have to go get the crazy little thing," the old woman mutters to herself. Her mind is a little vague from Scotch and lack of sleep. "Teenagers go off in their own little worlds sometimes."

She feels the need to clean and fix herself up before going down to get Marilyn. An old woman like her can look like a hag unless she takes care with her grooming. So she bathes and brushes her teeth, washes and sets her hair, sits under the hairdryer while she does her fingernails. She hasn't done them in over a year. The cuticles are a real mess. Then she begins to apply her makeup, very conscious that it's easy for a woman of her age to look like a painted old whore if her makeup is done poorly. Her hair has always been a problem.

The girls at the beauty parlor always dye it either too reddish or too black. It is thinning in the back, so she knows it flattens out ungracefully, but there is nothing left to tease and spray into any sort of fullness.

"What to wear, what to wear." She reflects with some mirth that she has been repeating the same double phrase upon approaching her closet since she was a girl of fourteen. Today she chooses her new pea green shirtwaist to which she adds a smart white neck scarf edged in the same pea green. She completes the ensemble with her white patent leather pumps.

A new man is at Marilyn's door. I see him standing there across the courtyard. He is holding a big bouquet of flowers. They are not all roses but luscious nevertheless. The man is handsome, tall and well-built, with sandy blond hair, a strong jaw and sensuous mouth. He knocks, he waits. I stand frozen behind my screen door to see if Marilyn will appear. I hear him calling to her: Marilyn! Then, through a window: Hey, you up yet? You home? He turns his back to the door. What an emotional young man. What passion. I can see from here how his jaw muscles are champing. He stands there for five minutes. He does not smoke a cigarette. Then he gives up. Pulls a flower from the bouquet and leaves it on the doorstep. He selects a red rose. He walks away, taking his bouquet with him.

I am living in obscurity now. Bouquets are nothing but mulch.

When I get to the basement room, Marilyn will not answer my knock. Poor Marilyn, I think as I sneak inside, afraid to turn on the lights. *Poor Marilyn*, and in this thought I would not be alone. She would become the smiling tragedy whose skirt waved delectably around her thighs, whisked aloft by the infernal wind that emanated from below. You, too, can forget your despair. On her picture with the dress blowing up she has scrawled a four letter word: *OOPS*. I slide down the hourglass in throes of gravity. I live in obscurity because it gets me tight.

I'm all dressed up to go nowhere. One must believe in gravity.

They are putting too much makeup on her in those

color pictures on the magazine covers. Trying to deflect the sexual aggression of men who would grind her into sand through no fault of their own, with long slow fucks. She is really nothing to me. I turn her over and read the advertisement on her back. I turn over the advertisement and admire the fact that she has such a perfect hourglass figure. She has a secret. I am that secret. I am the dark disturbed shadow of Marilyn Monroe. Men walk on me, that is, fuck. Come on in if you're not afraid of the dark. Turn me over. I'm not wearing any . . . lipstick . . . on my . . . sex appeal.

Dead Talk

Lynne Tillman

I am Marilyn Monroe and I'm speaking from the dead. Actually I left a story behind. I used to be jealous of people who could write stories, and maybe that's why I fell in love with a writer, but that doesn't explain Joe. Joe had other talents. I didn't even know how famous he was when we met. Maybe I was the only person in America who didn't. I was glad he was famous, it made it easier for a while, and then it didn't matter, even though we fit together that way. The way men and women sometimes fit together. It doesn't last. I got tired of watching television. Sex is important but like anything that's important, it dies or causes trouble. Arthur didn't watch television, he watched me. People thought of us like a punchline to a dirty joke. Or maybe we had no punchline, I don't know. Anything I did was a double entendre. It was different at the beginning, beginnings are always different.

Before I was Marilyn Monroe, I felt something shaking inside me, Norma Jean. I guess I knew something was going to happen, that I was going to be discovered. I was all fluttery inside, soft. I was working in a factory when the first photographs were taken. It was during the war and my husband was away fighting. I was alone for the first time in my life. But it was a good alone, not a bad alone. Not like it got later. I was about to start my life, like pressing my foot on the gas pedal and just saying GO. And the photographs, the first photographs, showed I could get that soft look on my face. That softness was right inside me and I could call it up. Everything in me went up to the surface, to my skin, and the glow that the camera loved, that was me. I was burning up inside.

Marilyn Monroe put her diary on the night table and knocked over many bottles of pills. Some were empty, so that when they hit the white carpeted floor they didn't make a sound. Marilyn made a sound for them, something like whoosh or oops, and as she bent over she pulled her red silk bathrobe around her, covering her breasts incompletely so that she could look down at them with a mixture of concern and fascination. Her body was a source of drama to her, almost like a play, with its lines and shapes and meanings that it gave off. And this was something, she liked to tell her psychiatrist, that just happened, over which she had no control. After three cups of coffee the heaviness left her body. The day was bright and cloudless and nearly over. She thought about how the sky looked in New York City, filled with buildings, and how that was less lonely to look at.

Marilyn just wanted to be loved. To be married forever and to have babies like every other woman. Her body, in its dramatic way, had other ideas. Her vagina was too soft, a gynecologist once told her, and Marilyn imagined that was a compliment, as if she were a good woman because her vaginal walls hadn't gotten hard. Hard and mean. But maybe that's why she couldn't keep a baby, her uterus just wouldn't hold one, wouldn't be the strong walls the baby needed. Marilyn's coffee cup was next to her hand mirror and she was lying on her white bed looking up at the mirrored ceiling. She was naked now, which was the way she liked to be all the time. When she was a child, the legend goes, she wanted to take off all her clothes in church, because she wanted to be naked in front of God. She wanted him to adore her by her adoring him through her nakedness. To Marilyn love and adoration were the same.

Marilyn took the hand mirror and opened her legs. Her pubic hair was light brown and matted, a real contrast to the almost white hair on her head, which had been done the day before. It was as if they were parts of two different bodies, one public, one private. My pubic hair is Norma Jean, how I was born, she once wrote in her diary. It was hot and the air conditioner was broken. She could smell her own smell, which gave atmosphere to the drama. Her legs were open as wide as they could go and Marilyn placed the mirror at her cunt and studied it, the opening into her. Sometimes she thought of it as her ugly face, sometimes as a funny face. She made it move by flexing the muscles in her vagina.

He said he'd marry me but now I know he was lying. He said I should understand his position and have some patience. After all he has children and a wife. I told him I could wait forever if he just gave me some hope.

Marilyn took the hand mirror and held it in front of her face. She was thinner than she'd been in years. Her face was more angular, even pinched, and she looked, finally, like a woman in her thirties, her late thirties. She looked like other women. The peachiness, the ripeness that had been hers was passing out of existence, dying right in front of her eyes. And she couldn't stop it from happening. Even though she knew it was something that happened to everyone, it was an irreparable wound. Her face, which was her book, or at least her story, did not respond to her makeup tricks. In fact, it betrayed her.

Marilyn needed to have a child, a son, and she wanted him with the urgency of a fire out of control. Her psychiatrist used to say that it was all a question of whether she controlled Marilyn or Marilyn controlled her. Marilyn always fantasized that her son would be perfect and would love her completely, the way no one else ever had.

Sometimes I meet my son at the lake. One time he was running very fast and seemed like he didn't see me. I yelled out Johnny, but at first he didn't hear. Or maybe he didn't recognize me because I was incognito. He was so beautiful, he looked like a girl, and I worried that he'd have to become a fag. Johnny said he was running away from a girl at school who was driving him crazy because she was so much in love with him and he didn't care about her at all. I asked him if she was beautiful and he said he really hadn't noticed. Johnny told me every time he opened his mouth to say something, she'd repeat it. Just staring at him, dumb like a parrot. As his mother I felt I had to be careful, because I wanted him to like women, even though I didn't trust them either.

Marilyn had asked her housekeeper to bring in a bottle of champagne at five every afternoon, to wash down her pills. And because champagne could make her feel happy. Mrs.

Murray knocked very hard on the door. Marilyn was so involved in what she was thinking about, she didn't hear. Marilyn was envisioning her funeral, and her beautiful son had just begun crying. There were faces around her coffin. But his was the most beautiful. No, Mrs. Murray said, he hadn't telephoned.

I told Johnny that more than anything I had wanted a father, a real father. I felt so much love for this boy. I put my arm around him and pulled him close. I would let him have me, my breasts, anything. He looked repulsed, as if he didn't understand me. He had never done this before. He had always adored me. Johnny wandered over to the edge of the lake and was looking down intently. I followed him and stared in. He hardly noticed me, and once I saw again how beautiful I was, I felt satisfied. Maybe he was too old to suck at my breasts. But I wanted, even with my last breath, to satisfy his every desire. As if Johnny had heard my thoughts, he said that he was very happy just as he was. He always lost interest anyway when someone loved him.

The champagne disappointed her, along with her fantasy. Deep down Marilyn worried that they had all lied to her. They didn't love her. Would they have loved her if her outsides had been different? No one loved Norma Jean. She could hear her mother's voice telling her, Don't make so much noise, Norma Jean, I'm trying to sleep. But it was Marilyn now who was trying to sleep, and it was her mother's voice that disturbed the profound deadness of the sleep she craved. If she couldn't stand her face in the mirror, she'd die. If they stopped looking at her, she'd die. She'd have to die because that was life. And they were killing her because she needed them to adore her, and now they wouldn't.

I hear my mother's voice and my grandmother's voice, both mad, and they're yelling, Save yourself, Norma Jean. I don't want to be mad. I want to say goodbye. You've got my pictures. I'll always be yours. And now you won't have to take care of me. I know I've been a nuisance and sometimes you hate me. In case you don't know, sometimes I hate you too. But no one can hate me as much as I do, and there's nothing you can do about it, ever.

* * *

Her suicide note was never found. Twenty years after Marilyn Monroe's death, Joe DiMaggio stopped sending a dozen roses to her grave, every week, as he'd done faithfully. Someone else is doing it now. Marilyn is buried in a wall, not far from Natalie Wood's grave. The cemetery is behind a movie theater in Brentwood.

* * * Marilyn Monroe * * *

Michael Lally

Everybody

         wanted her

                to do

a trick

for them

        but

        she had a trick of her own

that she wanted to do for   herself

      only

      she hated

      tricks

           (1969)

Untitled

Michael Lally

We've had too much of this patriarchal sentimentality.
—Ezra Pound

In 1913 Pound wrote to "Miss Monroe." In 1956 I pounded my pod, pulled my daisy, jerked off my prick and came all over my lean, white, teenaged thighs over a picture in *The New York Daily News* advertising a new movie by Marilyn Monroe. Waves of a new and old feminism swept various sectors and subcultures of the country between 1913 and 1956 and between 1956 and the present.
Many people drowned.
Many people were rescued.
Many people were cleansed and refreshed. Many other waves swept the country. Many other casualties of other waves succumbed to the feminist waves and vice versa. Horizontal oppression can be as evil or more so than vertical oppression. Miss Monroe, Miss Monroe, it was your eyes that attracted me, not your thighs. It was *my* thighs. What do I owe you now?

(1975)

Marilyn Gets a New Dress

Eleanor E. Crockett

Perry wasn't sleeping at all well. There was a little headache in the upper left cortex, just on the surface, but it wouldn't go away. It affected her nose, and the space between her eyes, all just on the surface, so that when she pressed lightly on these places, the headache temporarily subsided, but one couldn't fix lunch or brush one's teeth while performing acupressure, one hadn't enough fingers or arms. One couldn't go about in public with one's fingers splayed about one's head like a salamander. People would imagine something was wrong.

If only Marilyn would leave her alone, but no. Whenever Perry tried to fall asleep, Marilyn visited her. Even in waking moments, Marilyn was there. She obviously wanted something. Perry wished she'd come to the point, be more definite. The headache might decide to take up residence, like in her sinuses.

The first indication of Marilyn's presence was in a dream. Perry had gone to bed after watching a movie on television about mannequins. The boy in the movie fell in love with a mannequin who came to life at night, and the girl in the movie reminded Perry of Marilyn. The boy reminded her of Larry, her ex-boyfriend. The next morning, Perry had a headache wondering whether Larry preferred Marilyn Monroe to herself. Maybe he'd rather be somebody else's boyfriend, real or not. True, Marilyn was much prettier than she, with a sweeter tone to her voice, if it was her voice. But she couldn't be unkind to Marilyn, because she admired her too much. She could picture Larry with Marilyn, and the match pleased her. They looked good together.

Combing her hair that morning, it occurred to Perry that Marilyn was tired of being blond and would rather have straight brown hair like her own, but the little headache on top of her head gave a twinge, so she discarded that notion. Silly, she thought. Why would Marilyn want straight brown hair?

Maybe Marilyn wanted Larry. She hated that thought, so discarded it as well. No twinge. She felt relieved, and decided to give her hair a henna treatment. Not a red one, a conditioning one. But the headache continued to lurk, claiming a part in everything. Over breakfast, Marilyn said, "More Grape-Nuts."

How! I'll go to the mall today and see if anything turns up there, Perry thought. The mall was a good choice. The headache dimmed somewhat, enough for her to consider dressing up a bit. Why not? Dress up a bit, feel better, look better, go to the mall.

In the bathroom mirror, Perry regarded her lips. Dressing up implied lipstick and other makeup. Do I dare? She seldom wore makeup anymore; long ago as a student, then as a secretary she'd enjoyed the ritual, making herself "up." The idea was not to look like somebody you weren't, but to look more like who you were. Still, she felt different with makeup, as she felt different after straightening her hair. She understood it was a matter of habit, whatever you're used to. Used to, what a phrase. Now she was used to no makeup. With or without makeup, she scared herself in the mirror, like a child. She knew she and the reflection were not the same thing. She didn't know the reflection, she knew herself. Eyeliner and lipstick, lots of jewelry, were scary in a different way than the naked face, her naked body. It's what you're used to, she thought again. If her face changed in time, then why not change it at will, take charge? Most women enjoyed doing that.

"Try the red lipstick," suggested Marilyn.

"No, I won't. My mother told me in junior high that

red lipstick was for . . . that girls who wore red lipstick weren't respected."

"You're not in junior high."

"I might as well be. I like red lipstick, but only with red clothes."

"I like red lipstick."

"You are not I."

"I know. Pink lipstick is nice."

"I wear pink lipstick with pink clothes."

"Well, whatever shade you like. I never did my own makeup, I had a beautician."

"You see? Makeup is an art, not an ordinary practice for the ordinary or uninitiated person. Women spend too much time on it, in my opinion."

"What color do you prefer?"

"I prefer the color of my lips."

"So do you have a lipstick the same shade?"

"Yes, I have. It took me two years to find it."

"Then put that on. It seems pointless, though."

"I know what you mean. I'll put it on anyway; that's what dressing is, accentuating the obvious."

"Yes, you're right, absolutely," breathed Marilyn. "My manager told me that, and it always worked."

"I agree. For you it worked great, so why not for me?"

"You can't very well match your clothes when you aren't wearing any."

"And if you're wearing purple clothes, it's too scary in daylight to wear purple lipstick."

Marilyn shuddered. "Never in my wildest dreams have I worn purple lipstick. Have you?"

"Yes, when I'm feeling mean and want to scare people, to make them notice me, and prove how ugly makeup can be."

"You have to wear makeup in the movies, otherwise the lights wash out all your natural color."

"Yes, I know. And we're not in the movies, are we?"

"Daylight is just as cruel, especially in winter. I suppose that's why people get tans."

The conversation was inane, but it continued throughout Perry's toilette. Marilyn seemed to be trying to hold her attention, to her reflection in the mirror, probably. Perry decided to ignore the episode. In the spirit of cooperation, she splashed cologne on her neck, determined to banish that sultry mood of reflection. What now to wear? Better make it quick, her desire to leave the apartment was waning. She tried to recall her dream about Larry. Where had they been? Would she ever see him again? They'd parted two years before. It was in a mall, she was repeating the movie on television in her dreams. It wasn't important, but she longed for him. Marilyn might be Larry in disguise. They were both memories.

She regarded the clothes in her closet. The stretch pants insinuated themselves instantly—they were purple. All right, then, stretch pants. Marilyn approved. She slipped into them without thinking, and only noticed the line of her underwear later in the car. "Oh well, I don't care. I'll pretend I'm not wearing any, how terrible of me."

The mall was cool, as she knew it would be. People went to the mall in summer to cool off; the merchants counted on the heat. Her headache lay sulking in one corner of her brain. Marilyn was waiting for the right moment. It came as Perry swung into the parking lot. Waves of heat shimmied up from the pavement.

"A new dress," Marilyn's voice said.

"A new dress! Like I can afford one of those!" Perry replied.

"A new dress," repeated Marilyn in her kitten voice. "You heard right. I'm simply starving for one. This old rag I've worn for guess how long, two years."

"Two years, that's an odd number," answered Perry as they swung along the parklike esplanade. "You've been dead now at least twenty years."

"No, I haven't," Marilyn retorted, offended that Perry would bring up such a sordid fact. "I was in purgatory for simply ages. I only died two years ago, and now I'm forty-two."

Perry calculated. "That means twenty-four dead years for every one alive. Hmm."

"You're pretty smart," Marilyn said. "How do you know whether I meant forty-two living or dead years?"

"I'm going by the calendar," Perry said. "If you died two years ago by your own calculation, then by my calendar that's twenty-four." She was glad to discover that Marilyn couldn't read her thoughts unless she spoke them to her.

"Oh!" exclaimed Marilyn.

Perry's headache leaped to her attention. She was passing a Casual Corner outlet. "Oh, no, not that one, please." But Marilyn insisted.

"No, I refuse. I'm wearing this dress, even if I am buying it for you, and I prefer a more daring look."

"Bobby won't like it," murmured Marilyn.

"This dress isn't for Bobby, it's for Larry," Perry told her.

"Larry who, who is Larry? Oh, I know a Larry, Hagman. We did a movie together."

"This is a different one. You don't know him yet, but you will."

"Ooh, this is exciting!"

"Really? I'm glad. Now pay attention to me. Here's a boutique. I need you to help me decide which dress you want. This is going to be more fun than I thought."

"Me too," agreed Marilyn.

As they entered the boutique, Perry felt herself starting to perspire. It was the air conditioning, she knew, to which she wasn't accustomed. Larry would either like her in this new dress or she'd die choosing it. Just a minute, she thought. That sounds more like something Marilyn would imagine than something I would.

This was getting complicated. She stood gazing at the world of clothing and accessories, dazzled by the chaos of colors and patterns she saw. Nothing was wrinkled. Her mind wandered, collecting parties, bars, and other galas where she'd worn clothes similar to these. The parties invaded the boutique, spilling champagne and dripping marmalade.

Hurriedly she advanced to the nearest rack and flipped

through the doughnut of blouses outlining it. A red sequined number leaped to her touch, but when she pulled the hanger from the wheel, the blouse slipped off and fell to the carpet. "Oh, geez," she said aloud, glancing around to see whether anyone was watching her. It was a beautiful blouse, sheer red nylon sleeves embroidered with swirls of red beads, a bodice of red sequins laid in waves alternated with thin strips of a deeper red velvet. Kneeling, she retrieved the hanger and stood with it held against her collarbone. She saw red sand dunes glittering on her chest, or a maritime sunset.

"It's pretty, but it's too short for a dress," the dead movie star said.

Modesty, thought Perry. To Marilyn she said, "Styles change. They're wearing dresses shorter now."

"But not that short, I'm no dummy. With that on, a person could see a person's bum. Put it back." She hesitated. "I see something over there."

Perry held on to the blouse, but moved in the direction indicated by Marilyn. She remembered putting on makeup so long ago, musing about her friends, all the people she'd met and admired, wondering how to make herself look like them. She remembered choosing clothes with them in mind, then wearing them herself, whether or not they suited her, pretending they did.

This is kind of ridiculous, she thought, transporting the blouse past the boutique's hand-steamer, an appliance used by personnel to press garments newly released from their long journeys packed in boxes like sardines or lipstick, the red lipstick she tried so many times to wear, feeling like Marilyn, or trying to.

"Here is a dress like the one I wore in that film I made with Tony Curtis and Jack Lemmon. Did you ever see it? It was so thrilling to work with such great comedians, you know? I always thought I was a good comedian, comedienne. I learned a few things working with those two fellows. They were very amusing, don't you think so? Do you think I was funny? Couldn't I be funny if I felt like it? It was a little disturbing, all that deadpan stuff, you know if you're trying to make other people laugh, you have to keep a straight face yourself, otherwise people think you're just doing it for pleasure instead of for them. Those two guys were very good looking, too; of course, they weren't as good looking as me, which would have made it difficult. To be myself, I mean. I would have gotten mixed up. It would've been just too confusing, like a mirror."

Perry stood aghast. She'd never heard Marilyn open up so, talk so much inside her own head.

"Why are you talking so much? Don't you know I have to take responsibility here? I'm the real person, I'm the one paying for this dress. Now, let's try to concentrate, shall we?"

There was Mary and Marie. Perry thought of all the women she knew with names like Marilyn. Mary Ann, Mari, Mara, Lynn, Linda, Mariah, Margit. Did she also buy clothes for them? Did she have clothes in her closet at this very moment bought under their influence, their appearance, their name? Half Mary, half Lynn, Marilyn. Perry was lost somewhere inside, except for the very distinct *P.*

"I like this blue one, this casual, sight-seeing type of dress, how about you?"

"Yes, it's nice. Try it on. I'll go with you."

"Let's find a couple more first. If you had your own body, you could stay out here and look while I try them on. You could hand them to me. However . . ."

"Yes, the body. The hair, the face, and the body."

"They're all so different from mine, you see. Why did you choose me to inhabit, anyway?"

"I didn't choose you, silly, you chose me."

Now it was Perry's turn to say "oh." Perrylyn. Mary Perry. Marilyn Perry. All terrible. A salesgirl approached.

"Can I be of some help?" she asked.

"Yes, thanks. I'm looking for a dress, something different."

The salesgirl laughed. "They're all different here. We cater to the outrageous."

Perry blinked. Surely she hadn't said that. She'd said,

"We cater to the unique." Sales personnel were all so confident these days.

"Well, that's good," she said condescendingly. Marilyn might have said the same thing, adding kindly, "I think we're all unique, don't you?" Perry merely continued. "Something not too curvy, as you can see I'm kind of straight."

"You don't look so straight to me," said the young woman. "Plain or fancy, cute or sophisticated, flashy or calm? We have them all. This one, for instance, is very flattering. It seems to look good on just about anyone."

How nice for it, thought Perry. She followed the girl to a vertical rack with only four dresses hanging there.

"Fancy and sophisticated, I think. That's what I'd like to be. This one is too flashy and cute. It's very pretty, though." Perry felt a twinge of headache between her eyes. "Marilyn Monroe could wear that, not I."

"Oh, you think so?" The salesgirl replaced the dress.

"Yes, I do," said Perry. "I think a lot of these dresses were designed for Marilyn Monroe."

"Madonna, maybe," countered the girl. "Yes, that's probably true. I have something in this other line you might like, a Lauren Bacall or a Hepburn."

Perry didn't know whether she was being taunted or not. "Let's stick to the moderns. I agree with you. How about a Karen Black."

"Oh, tough." Another aberration. The girl had said simply, "Touché."

"Yes, like I said, sophisticated. No Basinger or Spacek."

"Nothing country, more urban."

"Exactly right."

The girl led her to a rack lining the wall. "How about this green?"

"That looks good." The dress was slim and well cut, a soft lawn. "I'll try that."

The girl selected the dress, cradling it in two hands. "Do you want to try that blouse, too? I'll put them in the dressing room for you."

As she departed, Marilyn spoke. "I like that green. I'll wear contacts with it."

Perry browsed the rack then turned to look through another one. A velour dress the color of blood hung hidden between two others.

"Yes, take that one," said Marilyn. "It's good for the zoo."

Perry laughed. "Marilyn, you *are* funny."

"This is a cheap boutique," said Marilyn, pleased with herself, "don't you think so?"

"Well, yes, but it's within my budget. I feel like rock 'n' roll, whaddya say, can you handle it?"

"I always preferred classical, but perhaps that's my training. You choose something you like. I know I'll look good in it."

"A dress is more disco or pop, though. How can a dress be rock 'n' roll?"

"I don't know. I never would have thought of it myself. If it were a concert, instead of dancing . . ."

"Good idea. I'll go with Cher. Let's see if there's anything like that in here. Purple or black, and rock 'n' roll is tawdry, something with things hanging off or pasted onto it."

"That sounds absolutely frightful!" Marilyn objected.

"That's it, frightful. But fun, funny."

"You mean humorous?"

"Yeah, humorous. Not serious."

"I always was accused of being too serious. You would be serious too, though, if you'd gotten involved in the kind of things I did. Against my will, too. Not that I was ever serious about anything . . . but myself. I was just trying so hard to have *fun!*"

"That's what I thought," Perry told her. "And I'm always trying so hard to be serious. Now don't you worry about anything. I know just what to do."

"You do?"

"Yes. See that little jumpsuit over there? Let's put that on."

"It's your body," said Marilyn more happily now. "I'll just have to trust you, I guess."

The salesgirl had put the chosen garments into a room and was busy now with another customer. Perry took a size-twelve jumpsuit from a rack loaded with similar costumes. It was white denim with silver studs, satin fringe above the bosom, and silver studs down the outer seam of the clamdigger legs. It was sophisticated and fancy, and maybe a tad cute. "We'll see."

In the dressing room Perry and Marilyn tried on all the clothes. First the green, but it was too Lauren Bacall. Then the velour, which was too simple and demanded more curves. Marilyn didn't object. Then the blouse, which was gorgeous. Perry put it aside. Finally, she slipped into the half-cowgirl/half-biker jumpsuit and fastened all the switches. The tassles swished menacingly. "This is it, I think," said Perry.

"I like it," said Marilyn. "It's good for the beach and for cocktails."

"You got it," replied Perry. "Now let's get out of here."

The jumpsuit was a reasonable price, designed as it was for young women. "If only it came in red," Marilyn started to pout.

"Oh, no you don't. Besides, I'm taking the blouse too, and it's red."

"So there," replied Marilyn. They were speaking the same language now.

The blouse cost as much as the jumpsuit. If only Marilyn were carrying some cash on her, thought Perry. But no matter, it was worth it. The cashier took her credit card and ran it through the nationwide gamut. Fortunately, it passed, clean as a whistle.

"If only I'd been wearing these clamdiggers when that draft came up through the grate, you know, on the street, then I'd never have got in so much trouble."

"Sure, but we wouldn't have that picture to remember, either. The world would be a poorer place."

"You really mean that?" asked Marilyn.

"You bet I do. A much poorer place. You have no idea how much that image means to the American public, and not just Americans."

"Oh, yes, I think I do," Marilyn whispered.

Perry's headache was gone.

Marilyn Monroe Returns

Robert Peters

Pensively she removes her slip and bra, removes
her silk net stockings.
She admires her milky skin
and the jounce of her calves.
She fondles her breasts.
They are far more delicious than Zsa Zsa's.
She never imagined she'd see birthday sixty-three.

She's aged little.
Yet, there are those indelible neck lines,
and her cheeks puff
as though her subcutaneous flesh was marshmallow.
There's a crease along her jowls.
Since she's utilized natural beauty secrets
always, she's no painted hag.

She laughs then weeps, with her legs ajar,
catching their image in a pink scalloped mirror.

She plans to attend
Mrs. John Wayne's Christmas bash
in *très chic* Newport Beach.
John Wayne was kind to her once, when she was down.
"Who needs Dasher and Dancer when you've got dashin' and
dancin'?" gushes the Society Columnist.
Widow Wayne must banish Gucci, her scruffy parrot (bless
him) to the master suite:

"You never know what Gucci is going to do
when people are around."
An elkhound pup has bitten Pilar
who wears Band-Aids on her arms.

Should Marilyn wear a trendy mumu or a gauzy number
suitable for a queen in *A Midsummer Night's Dream?*
She selects the dress she wore
standing over the hot air when the skirt flounced.
She said "Oops." Remember?

After her "suicide," Marilyn worked
in the artichoke fields.
She lived with migrants
eating frijoles and carnitas.
She stopped talking baby talk.
She tidied her men's lean-to, cooked a bit,
finally got a fourth wall and a bathroom,
and spent hours "improving" herself.
She read all of Dostoyevsky,
an author she admired when she strove
to be intellectual for Arthur Miller.
Static electricity always zapped her
whenever she touched *Karamazov.*
She dreamed of playing Grushenka on the stage.
She spent years reading Proust, Lawrence,
and a decade reading Shakespeare.
She'd hoped eventually to astound the world
by re-emerging, like Aimee Semple McPherson,
from the sea. She was a slow reader.

Marilyn was miserable over her comeback venue.
Why, oh, why, hadn't she phoned Miller or DiMaggio?
Joe never read much, but he was fun.
She missed Arthur's talk, shaping her brain.
"Don't move," shouted a photographer
as Marilyn floated in, in a mink stole.
He was snapping everybody's picture.

Once in the cha-cha room a déjà vu:
she was in an old Carmen Miranda film.
Pilar was an extra with no fruit on her head.
Her fingers protruded from her fist
like squiggly white potato roots.
Marilyn thrust her delicate hand,
still free of liver spots,
in Pilar's face, in disgust.
Pilar's mouth was a livid rose.
Wildly epileptic flute music
played to an ancient Greek diatonic scale.
S. Z. "Cuddles" Zakall laughed.
Drifting clouds were sheer panties
fulfilling fantasies of raunch.
A green moon dripped mint margaritas.
A swan of melting ice lost its honker and a left wing.

"Do I know you?" Pilar stared at Marilyn.
"I curse you with a seven-year itch," said Marilyn.

She hailed a taxi to Westwood Cemetery
where at 2 A.M., in sheen from streetlights,
she stood before her funeral niche.
Yes, there was DiMaggio's daily rose
hanging in its bronze heart-shaped holder.
She held the rose and wept.
Taking a key from her beaded purse,
she opened the tiny door, entered,
and willed herself into ash.
The next morning, groundsmen
picked a withered rose from the cement
and tossed it into a bin.
We'll never see the likes of Marilyn again.

Twenty-six Marilyns *or* An Alphabet Soup Full of Marilyns *or* Marilyn × 26 = *or* A Vignette Collage of Marilyns *or* Just Too Damn Many Marilyns

Michael Hemmingson

A = MARILYN THE ASSASSIN

The real reason why she disappeared was, yes, due to the CIA as some of the rumors and legends go, but not for the reason that she knew too much from those sweet postorgasm whispers by John and Bobby, nope. You see, the CIA approached her and said, "We want to recruit you as an assassin."

Marilyn went, "Oooooooh."

How did they know her deepest secret wish? Well, they

were the CIA, after all. More than anything—to be a singer, a sex goddess, and star—Marilyn always wanted to be a secret agent; better yet, an assassin.

So they sent her on missions, as herself (people merely believing that she was an impersonator of herself) or in disguises; to Eastern Europe, to China, to Cambodia, to Japan, to Latin America, and, finally, to the Soviet Union.

In the USSR, she was discovered. They held her prisoner: a spy, a killer. The only thing she confessed to them was that she'd once had an affair with John Le Carré. They didn't believe her. "How many people have you killed?" they asked. "Me?" said she, "would I ever kill anyone? Sweet little old me?"

A KGB officer fell in love with her. "I love you, too, comrade," she told him. He managed to break her out, and they both (fugitives now) ran away.

They ran away to Yugoslavia, passed themselves off as Croatians, and became farmers. They married, and it seemed like they would live happily ever after.

Then the Union collapsed; communism was on its way out. Marilyn discussed the possibility of coming out of hiding, returning to the States, writing a big book for, say, Warner or Random House, and making millions.

But the civil war in Yugoslavia made Yugoslavia Serbo-Croatian, and Marilyn, trying to flee the fighting, was struck in the back of the head by a stray impartial bullet.

B = M A R I L Y N   T H E
B A S K E T B A L L   S T A R

She was tired of being the most wanted woman in the world. She liked it once. Now she wanted something new. It took a lot of money—the stand-in body, paying off the right people for their silence. Marilyn arranged a sex change; but better yet, she arranged the color of her skin to be black. She also added a few feet to her height. When the operation was done, she looked like any young Black in the country. First, she went to New York to be a beat poet/playwright. That didn't work out because LeRoi Jones and James Baldwin had a monopoly on this, so she enrolled in college, was recruited by the basketball coach, a game which she discovered herself to be quite good at. Indeed, she excelled, and was subsequently recruited by a number of major league teams, where she soon rose to quick stardom.

Here I am again, she thought, a star.

She didn't mind.

She endorsed certain sportswear, she did commercials. She got married to a White woman who resembled herself when she was a White woman, but they didn't have any children.

Then she got AIDS. She didn't know where from. She hadn't been faithful to her wife on those many-city journeys during the basketball season (and she still had urges for men . . .).

The news of her disease became public. She was certain this would ruin her career. However, her popularity increased. "At least he's not afraid to admit it," people said.

A senator who was going to retire needed someone to take his place. He was, after all, a democrat. He approached her and said, "Do you want to be a politician?"

"Yes" she said, thinking of all the politicians she once knew in that other life.

NOTE: See P = Marilyn the Politician.

C = MARILYN THE CYBERPUNK

She wasn't buried. Her body was cryogenically frozen. In the year 2017, she was revived. Just her head, that is, for in 2001, due to certain cutbacks, that's all they were able to keep. The body was pickled in a large jar and purchased by a certain oil sheik.

The head was placed on an advanced, experimental artificial body, which wasn't unlike the body she once had. In fact, in certain ways it was better. There were many graduate students who lined up for the sexual experiments, but that's another story.

In this story, the United States was taken over by Japanese and German conglomerates. An underground resistance rose up in the country. The Japanese and German businessmen sent out killer robots, like the kind in *Terminator*, to obliterate this resistance.

Marilyn, using her skills as an assassin with the CIA, joined the resistance. She was so good that her essence and skills were downloaded onto a disk, which was transmitted via telephone system into the main network of the evil conglomerates. She was now a DNA cowboy, living in both the physical and digital world. As a virus in the mainframe the Japanese and German businessmen so relied on, she, as a new assassin, erased and scrambled much of the enemy's high-tech information, which was a direct result in the resistance overcoming the foe.

She was placed down in history for this.

D = MARILYN THE DYKE

Nevertheless, while she was known by many men to have the gift of giving great pleasures to these men, a certain number of women also knew the pleasures she had to offer. She was quite versatile, and her tongue was famous.

E = MARILYN THE EQUALIZER

She went to law school, graduated with good grades, and went to work for the district attorney's office in New York, specializing in violent and sexual crimes. She was a pretty good prosecutor, but once in a while a perp would go free on technicalities and witnesses who didn't show out of intimidation. In this job, she saw all the horrible things people do to one another in the big city. Dismayed that some rapists, sodomists, pedophiles, and serial killers were being let loose, she decided to take matters into her own hands. Going out into the savage night in a dark latex outfit and mask, she hunted down those who had gotten away and exacted what she felt to be justice.

"Now things are equalized," she'd say, after castrating some, or breaking arms and legs, or, once in a while, killing them.

She became quite a celebrity in the papers, this lone vigilante. In fact, Batman endorsed her, and pretty soon DC Comics will issue a limited miniseries of the crime-fighting adventures these two have shared.

F = MARILYN THE FRENCH RADICAL

She changed her name and origin, became a French natural, living in Paris and writing committed poetry. Marguerite Duras saw some of her stuff in a small journal and helped her get published, but she was still in obscurity. This didn't bother her. In the mid-eighties, she became a radical, joined up with the *Action Directe*, and was responsible for several bombings in the city. She hid out in Belgium for a while, then came back, where she landed a job at the Sorbonne teaching courses in feminist militant lit.

G = MARILYN THE GIANT

After a baseball star, a major playwright, and a President, she decided she had to go all the way and find odd lovers. So she got involved with a, well, let's call him a Mad Scientist. Unknown to her, he slipped a formula he'd been working on into her drink. This formula made her a giant. Marilyn was 900 feet tall, and she stormed through many cities, destroying things, until the United States called on Japan for help. Japan sent Godzilla and toy tanks to fight off Marilyn. Godzilla was hurt, but he was winning, despite the laser rays from Marilyn's eyes. The Mad Scientist didn't want to see his beloved hurt, so he injected her toe with an antidote and she shrank back to size, whereupon she collapsed. Godzilla and the toy tanks returned to Tokyo to fight Monster Zero, the three-headed space beast. When Marilyn woke up, she had no memory of the events.

H = MARILYN THE HOMOSEXUAL

See D.

I = MARILYN THE INVESTIGATOR

It was a rainy, gloomy night in the City of Angels, and she was thinking about calling the time card in, even though she was her own boss. She was wearing a snappy blue outfit, showing a lot of leg with dark stockings with clocks printed on them. She envied herself because she looked so good. She had her feet up on the desk, she was smoking a long cigarette, and she pulled a bottle of smooth Scotch from the desk drawer. She poured herself a shot, made a grimace as the booze went down, warming her deep. She had a second, and was feeling rather swell, when the office door opened and a man in a white suit and black trench stepped in, dripping all over the wooden floor. He removed his fedora, looking down at first, then looking up at her. The shadows from the streetlight outside crossed over his face.

"You're Marilyn the PI?" he asked.

"Could be," she said, putting her feet down and having another belt of Scotch.

"Do you always drink on the job?" the man asked.

"I'm not working right now," she said.

"You are," the man said, "because I'm hiring you and I don't like my employees drinking. Drinking is a bad habit; it's a moral sin."

"Listen, toots," she said, leaning forward and squinting, "let's get two things straight right off the noggin: one, I haven't accepted you as a client so therefore I am not working for you; and two, I drink when and where I damn well please because I happen to like good Scotch and this Scotch is quite good, which you would understand if you tried some but I'm in no mood to be hospitable and offer you any."

The man sat down. "My business is urgent."

Marilyn waved a hand. "They all say that."

"It's my twin brother."

"Your twin?"

"He's missing."

"What? You lose him?"

"Do you always have wisecracks to make?"

"I have to renew my subscription, but I have a few left."

"Maybe I came to the wrong place."

"There's the door, toots."

"But you came highly recommended," the man said.

"By who?"

"I can't say."

"You forget how to talk?"

"This source must be, for the time being, anonymous."

"You're being a cliché," she said.

"Pardon me?"

"I bet your brother made off with the family loot and that's why you want me to find him. You want the loot, you don't care about him."

"I do, very much." The man produced an envelope with pictures inside it. Marilyn took a look. A man who looked like this man was photographed in compromising new positions.

"He was getting involved with some bad people," the man said. "Doing this pornography stuff. I think they may have done something to him."

She shook her head. "I know what it is. You killed your own brother, and you need a fall guy. I go looking for him, come across his stiff, and get framed for the murder. Brother, you know how many murders I've been framed for? Another one would really make my day go all to hell."

"It's nothing as hard-boiled as that," the man told her. "I'm close to my brother and I'm worried about him."

Marilyn said, "I know what it is. There is no twin

brother. This is you in these pictures. Nice bod, by the way. But in my investigation, thugs will knock me around, I'll get threats in the mail, and you'll be leading me to decadence and depravity that I have yet to know the bounds of.''

"It's not like that at all," the man said, "I just want him found. I want to know that he's okay.''

"How long has he been missing?''

"Three days.''

"Maybe he went on a trip with someone.''

"No.''

"Maybe he doesn't want to be found.''

"That's not like him.''

"How do you know?''

"Because it's not like me, and we're twins.''

"Give me those pictures.'' She looked over the photos again. "Okay, I need a two-hundred-dollar retainer. I charge fifty bucks a day plus expenses.''

"Very well," the man said, bringing out the money. She counted it.

"How long will this take?''

"No more than a week,'' she said.

"This is where you can reach me," the man said, handing her a business card.

After he left, taking his rain with him, she put her feet back on the desk and had another shot of Scotch. Well, she had a case now. It was good to be among the employed.

J = MARILYN THE JUDGE

She worked her way up the ranks, and she was proud of herself. She went from being a small-claims court judge to a municipal and superior judge, and finally to a judge of the Federal District Court for the Southern District of California, where she managed to appoint several women as district magistrates. When an opening on the U.S. Supreme Court became available, her record and career came to the attention of the President. The President decided to make her a judge of the highest court, and the Senate confirmation sessions began. The interrogations were merciless. There were many hard-liners, not to mention many large companies with vested interests, who didn't want this sexy judge making decisions. The confirmations were televised, and the smears came in, especially from former law clerks who claimed that Marilyn had sexually harassed them. A number of men came forth and confessed, with downcast eyes, of the perversities Marilyn whispered into their ears.

One of them stated, "One time, it was my birthday, and she cornered me in a closet and sang 'Happy Birthday' to me in the most perverse and depraved way that I blush even recalling it now."

Many women wore buttons that said WE BELIEVE MAR-ILYN.

Men's-rights groups rallied not to have her confirmed into the Supreme Court.

But despite all the riffraff and bad press, Marilyn was placed in the high court, where, to this day, she hears and judges some of the most ground-breaking legal battles of the day.

K = MARILYN THE KOSINSKI

She was originally from Poland, during the Communist reign. By forging a number of documents and creating letters of recommendation from fictional people, she managed to obtain a visa to go to the United States, where she immediately requested asylum. The Communists tried to get her back. The CIA was interested in her. She told them things, and they asked if she wanted to be an assassin. "I was an assassin for you once," she said, "but I don't want to do that again."

"Okay," they said, "write books."

First, she wrote books filled with political essays. One day, she read a novel by Harry Crews and decided she wanted to write fiction. So she wrote fiction. The fiction was violent and autobiographical and received quite a bit of attention. She had her own table at Elaine's. She held office with PEN International. She told people many stories, of adventure and peril, toting them off as her real-life stories, which appeared also in her books. Some believed her, some didn't. She guest lectured at Ivy League schools. A scandal came out that she had never written her books; some say the CIA wrote them, some say her assistants penned them. She denied these rumors, and kept on writing good books.

L = MARILYN THE LITERARY CRITIC

As I am writing this text on a borrowed word processor, Marilyn comes bursting into my place—without phoning, without knocking, without a warrant—she barges right in. I jump up from where I'm sitting, spilling beer all over the pages I have printed so far, which I will now have to print again.

"Jesus, Marilyn," I say, "you scared the shit out of me!"

She's wearing a tweed skirt with matching jacket, leather belt around her waist. She has on smoke-colored stockings and black pumps. She also has gold-rimmed glasses and her hair is pulled back into a bun. I notice a sorority pin from Sarah Lawrence above her left breast.

She picks up the beer-soaked pages, reads through them, then looks at what I have on the screen, which is what you have just read prior to this, "Marilyn the Kosinski." She shakes her head and says to me, "You're nothing but a fraud, Michael. You call yourself an original? You're a literary thief."

"What?" I say, wiping up the spilled beer.

She throws down the pages. "This, you criminal. This piece of work, if you can call it that, is nothing but a half-assed rip-off of a Harlan Ellison story called *From A Through Z: In the Chocolate Alphabet.*"

"That's not true," I tell her, "and while I'll admit that I have *borrowed* the idea from Ellison, one of my favorite writers, by using the alphabet as a basis for sectioning off this text, there are fundamental differences. In Ellison's piece, each vignette was separate, on its own; all mine, in here, are thematically connected. Ellison wrote his story a long time ago, anyway, and for years I have been wanting to use a similar device, but didn't have an excuse for it. Besides," I add, "who are you to make a literary assessment of my work?"

"I review books for *The New Yorker* now," she says, chin up, grin on, "and I was the fiction editor of my college's literary review."

"Oh," I say.

"Well," she says, going to the door, "we'll have to see how it is when you're done. Toodles."

" 'Bye."

She's gone one minute and already I miss her.

M = MARILYN THE MARILYN

She's abducted by people in an alternate universe, a universe much like ours only they don't have a Marilyn in their universe and they want one. So they take ours, and she continues to be herself, but in that universe.

N = MARILYN THE NECROPHILIAC

I don't think we should get into this. Even *that* makes my stomach go uuuuuugggghh.

O = MARILYN THE OPTOMETRIST

I'm surprised to see that she's my eye doctor when I go for a visit.

"Your eyes are shit," she says.

"I know," I say, "it's all that reading."

"When's the last time you been to an optometrist?" she asks.

"Years and years," I say. "I used to wear glasses in junior high, but then my eyes got better so I stopped."

"They're not better," she says, "and you shouldn't have waited until you turned twenty-six."

"I'm sorry."

"I'm going to prescribe glasses."

"Yes," I say, "thank you."

"So," she says later, "what's the next installment?"

"You're in public office."

"Oh yeah."

P = MARILYN THE POLITICIAN

Okay, she had been a basketball star but now took the place of an incumbent senator, winning the race by a landslide, as they say. In Washington, she made many friends. In fact, some say she might run for President the next term. Let's see how she does until then, folks.

Q = MARILYN THE QUIET

She disappeared into Tibet, joining an obscure order of female monks. She took a vow of silence. If you go up into the Himalayas, and if you can find this distant monastery, you will see her there, in quiet meditation, the woman in the ivory tower, the secrets of the universe locked away in her mind. You will see bliss on her face.

R = MARILYN THE RAPPER

She's coming now, she's coming with a pow
She's big and strong, ain't gonna be long
Till you see with me you see what I see
Homes, it's the White girl who raps
Raps raps raps
Ain't no taps, the White girl that raps

She's in the big city
She ain't takin' no titty
This bitch ain't up for grabs
This bitch ain't takin' no nabs
Homes, it's the White girl who raps
Raps raps raps
Ain't no taps, the White girl that raps
Smokes no dope and sucks no dick
'Cuz she got the hope and a major flick
She's the Hollywood star
The madame of the bizarre
She's the one you'll spot
Some like it hot
I say, man, check this bitch out
She makes me scream and shout
She's the White girl who raps
Raps raps raps

S = MARILYN THE STREETWALKER

Burke drove across the Brooklyn Bridge and back into Manhattan, where he came across a streetwalker who looked familiar. He lit a smoke, then rolled down the window of his car. "Over here," he said.

She walked over. Dark circles under her eyes.

"So what you want?" she said. "Some head?"

"No."

"A fuck?"

"No."

"Look here," she said, turning, patting her rump, "look at that ass. Isn't that a nice ass? It's a sweet ass. You want to fuck my ass? You can fuck my ass, give it to me Greek, but it'll cost ya extra."

"No," he said.

"Come on," she said, "it's cold, biz has been slow, and if I don't bring in some cash my pimp's gonna beat me bad."

"Get in," he told her.

She got in.

He drove.

"I need money," she said.

"I want you to get off the streets."

"Funny."

"I can help."

"Why would you want to help?"

"I just do."

"What? You do this all the time?"

"Sometimes."

"Who are you?"

He shrugged.

"I'm old." She started to cry. "I can't be working the streets anymore."

"I know," he said.

"I used to be the biggest star in the world," she said.

"So have we all," he said.

T = MARILYN THE TOMB

What I am about to tell you is absolutely a true story, not the fancies I have been giving you here.

This was about five years ago. My friend Chris and I drove up to L.A., to Westwood Cemetery, where they have all these famous people buried. He wanted to see the tomb of Buddy Rich, the jazz drummer, who had died not too long ago. Chris was a drummer himself, and he admired Buddy Rich, had gone to see him play many times. I had seen Buddy Rich too, and was flabbergasted at the man's talent.

Chris did something that must be preserved in words: he played a Buddy Rich song with drum sticks on Buddy Rich's tomb. People passing by looked on with odd expressions, but Chris ignored them, playing away.

Walking around, we came across the tomb of Marilyn Monroe. Chris wanted a photo of this, so he took one. It was sad to see that the roses at her tomb were wilted, dead.

Later, Chris called and said, "Mike, my God, you have

to see these pictures from our L.A. trip, you have to see this *one*."

The picture he was referring to was, of course, the one of Marilyn's tomb. In this photo, the roses were not wilted and dead, but quite blossoming and alive, and on the gray slab that held her name, there was the faint imprint of full red lips. I'm not lying. They were there, in the picture. The only thing was, this wasn't what we saw when we were there, this wasn't it at all.

U = MARILYN THE UFO

Along with Elvis, she has been spotted all over the world inside flying saucers.

V = MARILYN THE VAMPIRE

Of course, she had to be a vampire.

Being a vampire was an aspiration of hers ever since the early eighties, when she'd go to goth clubs in New York, where people dressed all in black, wore pasty white makeup and dark lipstick, and the DJs constantly played Bauhaus's "Bela Lugosi's Dead." She knew she had to be a vampire after a strange encounter with Peter Murphy, the singer for Bauhaus, and a subsequent move to New Orleans, where she was an assistant to Anne Rice for a while.

She took a trip to Romania, hoping to find her vampire. She did not.

She looked high and low, hoping to be seduced and changed. This did not happen.

So she said the hell with it, started to seduce men, and bite into their necks and suck blood.

She didn't like the blood at first; it was a taste to acquire. She loves it now.

She is always thirsty.

She sleeps in the day.

Men are not safe.

This will scare the hell out of you.

Now in trade paperback.
First print run of 35,000 copies, floor display available.
Foreign and movie rights sold.
Endorsed by Clive Barker.
Major advertising, ten-city author promo.

W = M A R I L Y N   T H E   W I L D

Actually, that's the title of a novel by a great writer named Jerome Charyn.

X = M A R I L Y N   T H E   X E N O M O R P H

Sigourney Weaver didn't get the part as Ripley in *Alien*. Marilyn did. The story line was different, too. Marilyn's character is transformed into an alien, starting as a small creature first, then changing ever-rapidly into a huge monster. This is, by the way, the director's original cut, soon to be released in all major theaters near you.

Y = M A R I L Y N   T H E   Y A D D O
R E S I D E N T

It took her a number of years to make a small name for herself, writing poetry for obscure photocopied magazines, then in well-established literary quarterlies. Her first book won an award from a southern university and they published the book, gave her five hundred bucks. Not very many people read the book, but she did get a grant from the NEA as well as some stays at writers' colonies, particularly Yaddo.

At Yaddo, she sat in her room and wrote, sipping white wine. She sent her manuscripts, each day, to every place she could find, and she was, by this virtue, more published and widespread than Lyn Lifshin.

She had a few affairs with some other poets and one painter at Yaddo, telling them it was just for the moment. "I

must move on," she said to them, "and write more poetry."
>She wrote poems about these lovers and others.
>She wrote a suite of Yaddo poems.
>They were published.

Z = MARILYN THE ZYGOTE

Happily in her mother's womb, she grows. Even at this stage she knows she is destined for greatness; she's going to have an impact on the world, and any other worlds to come.

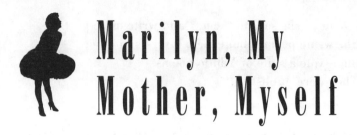

Marilyn, My Mother, Myself

Gregg Shapiro

Ever since I told my mother I was gay, eight years ago, she had taken it upon herself to buy every Marilyn Monroe T-shirt, knickknack, poster, baseball cap, photograph (some autographed), calendar, greeting card, book, audio recording, videotape, engagement book, ceramic pin, button, Franklin Mint doll, and Bradford Exchange limited edition collector's plate she could get her hands on and present it to me.

"I saw this in the window at the Artvark on Broadway," she'd say as she'd thrust a square box wrapped in Marilyn-standing-over-the-subway-grating wrapping paper at my chest, "and couldn't remember if you had this or not."

"A Marilyn's-face ashtray. Thanks, Mom," I'd say, trying to sound like a kid on a commercial who had just been served a plate of his favorite macaroni and cheese shapes.

Still, I couldn't help but wonder whether or not a real fan might find flicking ashes and extinguishing lit cigarettes on Marilyn's birthmark or ruby red lips a bit objectionable or sacrilegious. At least she hadn't yet come across a Marilyn Monroe commemorative pillbox. That would have been too much, even for her.

Her quest, it seemed, was eternal. She ventured, on her own (my father refused to be a party to her obsession), to parts of the city she never before knew existed, to find the missing pieces that would make my Marilyn collection complete. Dressing down and clutching her purse to her chest, she'd drive to the houses of other collectors living in the depths of the South Side, in Aurora, even as far west as Rockford, just so my already Marilyn-cluttered apartment could look more like a lost room at the Field Museum.

Each November 1, my mother tried unsuccessfully to conceal her disappointment when I told her that I'd attended yet another Halloween party not dressed as Marilyn Monroe. When I got a kitten and named it Tallulah, I sensed a strain in my mother's voice when we spoke on the phone or gathered for family functions and holidays during the following months.

I'd been toying with the idea of telling her that I was planning on leaving all of the Marilyn memorabilia to her in my will. Not that I was planning on dying anytime soon, but you never knew. Look at Marilyn; dead in the prime of her life.

Things could be worse, I supposed. What if she'd taken the Judy Garland angle? Or the Liza Minnelli approach? Barbra Streisand wouldn't have been half-bad, but I'd already managed to cover that territory on my own.

I couldn't even get a typical tourist postcard from any of the exotic places my mother and father visited since my father's retirement. Somehow, my mother managed to find postcards with pictures of Marilyn Monroe on them in every foreign port she'd visited. I never knew Marilyn Monroe was so well traveled. But there she was, leaning out of a window, walking on a beach, eating a carrot in bed. Sending me her (and my parents') greetings from Corfu, Belize, Tegucigalpa, Rio de Janeiro, Montevideo, Nice, and Samarkand.

On a domestic trip to Los Angeles to see my father's younger brother and his third wife, my mother insisted on making her umpteenth visit to Marilyn's gravesite at Westwood for more snapshots. It was the thirtieth anniversary of her death, my mother exclaimed, how could she not pay her respects and shoot a roll of film for me, her only son, who was pining away for the tragic but legendary movie goddess?

The thing was, I wasn't even a fan of Marilyn Monroe's "body" of work. The only movie I'd ever seen with her in it was *All About Eve* (Bette Davis is a different story altogether!), and I've been told it's one of Marilyn's early, smaller roles. Honestly, I couldn't tell *The Seven Year Itch* from a rash.

Just when I thought I'd reached the end of my frayed rope and considered faking a pills-and-booze suicide in my parents' bed (*Harold*, from *Harold and Maude*, had more influence on me than Marilyn Monroe ever did, Mother, if you're paying attention), I came up with the next best thing— a Marilyn Monroe tattoo. Why not? Everyone else, from celebrities to nobodies, seemed to be doing it, so why shouldn't I? Besides, my mother hated tattoos. I think it had something to do with some of her relatives, who had survived the Nazi concentration camps and had the numbers on their arms to show for it.

I, however, hated pain, and opted for a temporary tattoo. It was slightly more complicated than the lick-and-stick tattoos I used to get in boxes of Cracker Jack or from gumball machines, but I was certain that it would do the trick. The guy at the tattoo parlor guaranteed that it would last two weeks, through showers and saunas, hurricanes and tornadoes.

After the smiling-Marilyn-with-windblown-hair tattoo had been on my left bicep for a few days and the wrinkles had smoothed out, I invited my mother over for lunch. I used the excuse of wanting to show her how nicely her latest Marilyn "find" fit into the installation. She insisted on referring to my apartment as the "Norma Jean Shrine," to which I usually nodded my head in vague agreement.

I was wearing a muscle T-shirt that had been silk-screened with Marilyn in sunglasses and said PROVINCETOWN on it. For some reason, my mother stationed herself on my right side, when she came in and handed me her Indian blanket jacket, which I hung on my Marilyn coat rack (a *Home-Consumer Network* close-out). When we moved into the kitchen, laden with Marilyn potholders and trivets, aprons and coffee mugs, I positioned myself to her right and flexed my left arm.

Instead of swooning and asking for a cold compress for

her forehead and a place to sit down, she oohed and aahed, as if she were having a private audience with the Hope Diamond.

"Just don't show your father," she said in her most conspiratorial voice. "You know how *he* feels about tattoos."

First Authentic Star of the New Cinema

Taylor Mead

Marilyn Monroe killed herself
and I am shook up
a little didn't know her
well but looked into
her face once saw
nice open direct intelligent
girl sweet liked her in
Niagara great a child
original of Nature pushed
around because of it
especially when very young
her father was an ass
like most fathers are
She became an undulating
tender figure but figurine
to others and then the
mental merchants started
on her with their
Stanislavsky forcing her
to read his dull
works and
trying to help her make
her into an acting machine
when the method was

already undulating
gorgeously from her
every pore and no one
could have used it less.
Leave her alone—just shower
her with gifts.

*

I'm alive, I'm alive, I'm alive,

*

She is gone
She's really gone
She's made it off of
the planet.

*

Oh ephemeral Marilyn Monroe,
Oh ephemeral life,
oh ephemeral 20th Century Fox,
oh ephemeral me.
oh ephemeral you

*

I don't blame Marilyn Monroe for killing herself—what use is
it making movies for a bunch of gum chewing, gum popping,
popcorn crunching, candy-bar wrapper crumpling, mutter-
ing, banal talking during movies slobs.

*

radio commercial: "Nine out of ten Hollywood stars eat Cad-
illac Dog Food."

*

if nothing else my fame will teach people that anybody might
be anybody.

*

I am a fucking movie star. I've got two movies playing simultaneously on Manhattan Island, so blow blow blow

*

United States won't have come of age, humanity won't have
come of age until people can go to a theater and see anything
on earth, fucking, pissing, shitting, blowing.

*

This has been an impossible life, you understand?

*

the pain to the heart so great and the mind races to rationalize but never makes it and the effort screws you up.

*

speculating on what you might have done is utter vanity.

*

Acceptance Night at the Academy Award
I'm going to grope Oscar on the dais
I'll finger him and say "what a build"
I'll trot down the aisle with Elizabeth Taylor on one arm and Lee Strasberg on the other.

*

(ran out of money for the typewriter)
I think Marilyn Monroe needed the Method like Frank Sinatra needed "A Hole in the Head."

*

You know that's the universal rule in United States—No Dancing—mentally, physically, this country is so obtuse.

*

I'm waiting for Antonioni to phone.

*

There is no answer—that's the joy of it all

*

Marilyn had a record player, I don't know why she went and killed herself

*

I only go to see my own shows (movies)—It's the only time the audience is quiet and respectful.

*

while wealthy people commit suicide I twiddle my thumbs in degenerating idleness enforced by lack of money.

*

I may be the new Marilyn Monroe

FROM Life After Death

Susan Compo

Nobody knows Zelda Zonk's real name and in truth she's had so many that, if strung together like party lights, they'd make her sound like some extreme form of English royalty. Her present one, Zelda, was an alias often favored by Marilyn Monroe when she was in her self-portrait phase. Norma Jean would draw pictures of her body, oddly, all sharp lines, and then obliterate her face.

Zelda worships Marilyn Monroe of late and thinks herself the only one who really understands her. Zelda can talk to Marilyn, help her, as she summons her reluctant ghost to slummy, flat, poverty-row Hollywood from which Marilyn tried so hard to escape. Zelda believes that one day she'll find Monroe's mysterious ruby red diary and sees it in a vision, in a shoe box all tied up with shoelaces.

Zelda is going out tonight, a warm, lifeless night, to a trendy rock club that is sort of a mock English pub. The Fan and Flames has a painted sign out in front so the illiterate won't miss the symbolism, but because it's dark no one can see it anyway. Zelda wants everyone there to know that she's Marilyn's only true fan, that she has suffered absolutely for her painstakingly platinum hair and her *Seven Year Itch*-y dress.

Orange, a local celebrity, deejay, and record store owner, is holding court in a corner of the club, telling his admirers why he won't honor Elvis Presley with a window display on the King's birthday—which happens to be the same day as David Bowie's. Orange's equally flamboyant wife, Cruella, is known for her red fingernails and hair plus her sharp wit that strikes as expediently as a letter opener. She's sitting next to Orange and waiting for the right moment when she can breathe in deeply and make her announcement. She finds it and says, "What I always hated the most about Elvis," she pauses to look over at Zelda, "and Marilyn Monroe for that matter, is that they were basically low-life white trash hicks masquerading as something else but never really succeeding. That's why they came to such bad ends."

"Great," says Orange. "Hey, what do you say to that, Zelda? Cruella's calling Norma Jean white trash."

Zelda shrugs and dismisses the whole thing as pretend-salon banter. She figures they rehearse this stuff while they're doing their hair. She walks into the next room which has a lower ceiling and sees the stage is being set up for a band. A roadie with magenta hair (no trace of nature) and ermine-colored skin asks her if she's looking for someone.

"No, no. Who's playing tonight?"

"Orphan Charm. They're kind of glam." He wrinkles his nose.

"Oh." Zelda turns and starts to walk away.

"Hey, don't leave," calls the roadie, whose name is Vex. His real name is Asunción but he gave it up long ago since it really didn't suit the scene. Vex was a punk-rock name which is not where he is now. It doesn't match his present David Bowie/Ziggy Stardust incarnation but he is still known by it. He thinks Zelda would make a very good Angie Bowie for him, considering her platinum hair.

"I've just got to go to the bathroom," Zelda says. "Maybe I'll see you later." She goes to the ladies' room and has to fight several boys for a position at the damaged, broken mirror, portions of which appear to have been whitewashed. She feels the terminal boredom of the club and decides to go home.

Vex is guarding the back door in case anyone tries to steal the band's equipment. He sees Zelda attempting to make her escape. "Hey, blondie, blondie, wait!" he shouts, like a truck driver. "At least let me give you my phone number."

Something about his eyes makes him look like a fifties film star (they look like they could cut glass), Zelda decides, so she says okay. She fixes on his flaming hair as he writes his number on a matchbook.

"Are you parked very far away? Because I can walk you to your car if it's not that far."

They go to her Valiant and he stands by the passenger door, twisting the toe of his silver boxing boot into a stream of ants.

Zelda looks down until his action registers. "Stop that!" she screams. "You're killing them! You're killing them and they're helpless and innocent!"

"Okay, okay, sorry," he says. "I'm sorry to upset you."

"I just can't stand animals being hurt," she explains.

"I said I was sorry."

"Well, please be." She is rubbing her eyes. "Say, are you a big Bowie fan or something?"

"Yeah, but—"

"I mean it's funny because, well, usually with Bowie fans they try to keep up with the latest image and you're, you know, at least ten years behind."

"I know, I know. But you see, I think the thing about being a fan is like knowing when to freeze, like cryonics. You have to know when to thaw, too. It's like playing statue in the schoolyard."

More rhetoric, Zelda thinks, annoyed, as Vex leans her against the car door. "I dropped out of school," she tells him, "and anyway I have to get going." She turns away as he tries to kiss her.

At six A.M. the next morning Zelda's phone rings. It is a woman from the Living Dolls Casting Agency, for which she works as an extra. Will she, the voice wants to know, report to this fifties-style diner and dress in the period?

I could have starring parts, Zelda thinks, if I didn't live so much at night and my complexion were better. She turns on her curling iron and takes coffee and Vivarin. Walking across the floor of her tiny apartment, she goes to open a crusty Venetian blind and let in a line of light. She doesn't bathe, because, like Marilyn, she's not all that clean, but when she looks at the clock she jumps, since unlike Marilyn she can't afford the luxury of being late.

"You look like you just got up," says her contact at the diner as he gives her some forms to sign, which she does with a flourished script.

"Zelda! Zelda!" calls Cruella, whose trademark red hair is tied back in a taut ponytail. She is hard to recognize in ordinary makeup. "I'm glad to see you. Listen, I'm sorry about what I said last night. About Marilyn."

"Quiet, girls, please," says a man.

On her way home that night Zelda stops at a bar and has a martini. She thinks of Vex, of how she liked his icy gray eyes, and she decides to call him. She starts to leave a message on his machine but he cuts in. He's screening his calls like a superstar. Vex asks Zelda if she wants to stop by but explains that he has a rehearsal later that night.

"Are you in a play?" Zelda asks.

"No, no. I'm in a band called 5-Years. I'm the singer."

She drives her Valiant up his steep street and goes up the steps to the ornate Queen Anne house. The pale green shutters look as if they were crocheted. At the casement glass front door a dark-eyed child tells Zelda to go downstairs by pointing to the ground.

Vex opens his door and as Zelda enters his basement apartment she feels uneasy, like she's stepped into the belly of a piñata. Turquoise and pink *papier mâche* skeletons and devils, black-and-white coffins and skulls dance suspended on strings from the ceiling. The walls are covered with religious icons, sacramentals, novena cards, and crucifixes. A glass case displays a collection of faded *santos*. Posters break the religious zeal: Zelda recognizes David Bowie (as Ziggy Stardust), Sid Vicious, and Elvis Presley, but has to read the border to get Rudolph Valentino.

"Where'd you get all this stuff?"

"You like it? Let me show you my favorites." Vex

leaves the room. He returns with two intricately painted staffs, one of which he hands to Zelda. It is weighty and has a sharp gold tip.

"Now take this one," he commands.

She takes the other and gasps. "It's light as air!"

"They're props," he says. "From the original *Ten Commandments*. The light one is called the 'hero' 'cause it's for the star to use, to make him look tougher. The heavy ones are for everybody else."

"How'd you get these?"

"I stole them from the Studio Museum when I was working up there with sound equipment. I do that sometimes."

"You're lucky you didn't get caught," says Zelda.

"Yeah, well. Do you want a beer or something?"

"Okay."

He gets her a Corona and motions that she sit on the overstuffed couch. His coffee table is made from a tombstone.

"Tell me about yourself," he says.

"There's not really anything to tell." Zelda rarely speaks about her pre-Marilyn life. "How long have you lived here?"

He thinks for a moment. "About six years. I was measuring it by what job I had when I moved in."

"Oh." She notices a framed photo above the heater. "Is that you?"

"Yeah, me in my Sid Vicious days."

Zelda walks over to get a closer look. "Is that girl really Nancy Spungen?"

"Her? No. That was my girlfriend at the time. It's a pretty good likeness, though, isn't it?"

"I guess so. Are you religious or something?"

"I used to want to be a priest," Vex says. "I come from a hard-core Mexican Catholic family. Like my real name is Asunción." He exaggerates the *u*.

"What happened?"

"I woke up."

Zelda draws on her beer and goes back to the couch. The phone rings but Vex doesn't answer it and out of deference to Zelda he doesn't even bother to check who it is.

He reminds her, "You haven't told me anything about yourself."

"Yes, I did. I told you there was nothing to tell."

"For instance, what bands do you like?"

"Oh, none, really. It's not my scene."

Vex laughs. "Oh, come on. I don't buy that for a minute."

"Well, never buy what you can't afford." She gets up abruptly, her stiletto heels scratching the grooves of his hardwood floor like a record needle. "Anyway, I'm going to leave since you're not going to listen to me or take me serious."

"No, wait," he says. "I like your hair."

Zelda glares at him.

"How long have you had it like that?"

"I have no idea. This is the way I have it now. You of all people should understand that. This is where I've *frozen*."

Her sarcasm stuns him. "Look," he says, "why did you come here?"

"You invited me."

"Cut the cute replies, sweetheart," he says, undoing the long fringed scarf he wears around his neck. He loops it around her, pulls her close and into his bathroom. Hairspray, bottles of dye, and glitter are on the counter and spilled over the tile floor so that it looks like Hollywood Boulevard. "Listen," he says, "I don't know who you are or where you came from but stuff like that is just window-dressing anyway. All I know is I wanted to talk to you, to see you in the mirror with me. Look." He pulls her head up.

Zelda looks at her reflection and is relieved to see that the resemblance to Marilyn is there. But Vex is not quite right, she thinks. Unless she can change him, and she knows he's changed before.

Zelda goes home that night and finds Whitey, her cat, waiting for her at the front door. She feeds him and then gets ready for bed. She phones Cruella but the line is busy so she calls Vex and hangs up when the machine answers.

After Zelda gets into bed she lies in her last boyfriend's

spot. He was a tall boy who played baseball in college and signed with a major league's farm team (he is a pitcher). Then she hurls as if thrown back into her own space.

She can't sleep. She hears someone doing their laundry and she tries to change the sound of the washer and dryer into the hum of ocean waves.

Zelda thinks, if only I had some Nembutal. She gets out of bed and puts on her white, knee-length terrycloth robe. She's going to call on Marilyn.

The first thing she does is take the phone off the hook so no one will interrupt her concentration. Then she sits on the edge of her bed and starts to think until her forehead hurts.

The water's roar gets as loud as Niagara Falls and then tapers off to a hyped-up hum so Zelda can barely hear Marilyn's soft, faded-photo voice. She sees Marilyn standing on a bluff overlooking Santa Monica beach, her champagne-colored hair blown back by the wind. Marilyn's wearing sand white matador pants and her skin is the color of moonlight. She's both a young model and a tired star. She's very sheer and wears Plexiglas, platform-wedged shoes.

"I'm trying to reach my locksmith," Marilyn says. "He's close by." She drops the coin she intended for the pay phone and it falls into the sand, which has shifted directions with the wind.

Zelda gets a paper from her nightstand to write this down.

"Let me go," says Marilyn but not, Zelda thinks, to her. Zelda concentrates. "The diary, Marilyn, the red diary."

"That man," she whispers, "on the corner knows."

Zelda jumps up. "The coroner?" But Marilyn's gone, vanished as if she hadn't signed off but just put the phone receiver down.

Zelda's filled now with a loneliness and confusion as to her next step. How will she get to the coroner—while she's still warm, that is? She walks over to close a window because a Santa Ana wind has started to blow.

The phone rings as she hangs it up and Zelda nearly jumps out of her skin. It's Vex who just wanted to say hi, so

Zelda says hi, distantly, with the certainty that from now on each time they speak or get together they'll be more and more uncomfortable, for that's the nature of love.

When she falls asleep Zelda dreams about the diary. That it's been left somewhere in the rain and the ink is running and dripping like the blue blood from a fine-point pen.

FROM The Angel Carver

Rosanne Daryl Thomas

Though Lucille had entwined herself ever more in his life and the life of his angels, the shoe man knew he was losing her. It was an elusive loss. Not the usual thing. It wasn't the same as losing Angela or Angie, Mrs. Rice, or Leopoldine. And it had to do with Buddy. Naturally, the shoe man assumed Buddy and Lucille were lovers. When he pictured their loving, which he could not help doing, he pictured it in the way he knew, the way he and Angela had been together. After forty years, so many years, the touches, sighs, shudders were still imaginable to him, and when he imagined them, and Lucille, and Buddy, he found himself adding a second beer to his traditional nightly one. In his innocence, he imagined that someday Lucille and Buddy might marry and have a family. It took two beers not to think about it. But even after two beers he still thought about the main thing, the real loss.

Lucille was not Lucille anymore.

Lucille's Marilynization was along the lines of a living miracle, a miracle with frighteningly divine results, a miracle in which nothing divine was involved. He'd never seen anything like it. Though he called her Lucille and she answered to that name, she called herself Marilyn, and from what he could see and hear, she was practically right. She'd bought herself another pair of contacts, blue-gray this time. The exact shade, the right shade, according to Buddy. Under Buddy's tutelage, her voice had evolved into a sugar-crisp whisper. The way she walked was different. It wasn't a walk anymore, It was a white ship at sea. It was a rolling wave. The cherished feeling that he might be her father or even her grandfather curled in and browned at the edges, tainted by self-disgust and confusion. How could his gut not go tight as she passed when every step she took was a seduction? When her dresses squeezed her breasts in front and limned the furrow in her bottom in back? Was it an apricot, he wondered, and then he hated himself for the thought. A peach? A sweet nectarine? Any taste of summer fruit set him wondering, and fruit was something he could not resist. It was hard not to linger outside the bathroom door and breathe the sweet steam that came from her shower until his face was dappled with sweat. It was hard not to want to feel her paling skin with his hands and his mouth. It was hard for things to be the same when they weren't.

At a certain point the shoe man thought, with enormous relief, that her changes had gone as far as they could go. What with beating Robert Smythe by unanimous decision in the second Marilyn Monroe contest she had ever entered, winning fifteen hundred dollars' prize money, the traditional armload of red roses and an opportunity to sign a contract with Resemblances as a Marilyn look-alike model, even Lucille briefly dared to be happy with the current version of her self, until.

Until Buddy said the watery word, nice. Buddy hailed a taxi for the shoe man, who wasn't surprised when Lucille said she'd be home later.

Lucille and Buddy walked nowhere in particular, said nothing much until Buddy drawled, "It's . . . nice. But hardly enough."

"What do you mean nice? It's wonderful. Resemblances wants me. I'm good enough for them and that's good enough for me," Lucille argued, quickening her step and realizing that her feet didn't hurt in her high heels. That was thanks to the shoe man. He appreciated her.

Buddy shrugged. "Then I'm wasting my time," he said, stepping to the curb and raising his arm although there was no cab within blocks of where they stood.

Lucille pulled his arm. He resisted. "Wait. Why?"

"Because they're in it for the money. It's a business. They take a percentage. That's why. Because they do crummy little look-alikes. If that's what you want for yourself, we part here. I don't give a shit about amateur Marilyns and goddamn phony Elvises. Life's too short for waxwork imitations and if that's what you want to be I don't give a shit about you. But it's a goddamn pity, because I do the real thing and you could have been it. Instead, what? You want to be, what? Some imperfect little almost." Buddy spat on the ground. "And they'll let you and they'll tell you that you're good. That's because they don't care about you." A cab stopped beside them. "And I do."

Maybe it was that he said he cared. Who knows? Instead of breaking free on the spot, Lucille wrapped her arms around him until her muscles strained and stood between him and the door handle. "What do you mean could have been?"

She wept as he ripped the Resemblances contract into many more pieces than were necessary to destroy it and let it fall into the black gutter, but she wept silently. "I'll take care of you," he murmured, reaching under her platinum hair to stroke her aching neck. He didn't want to take her to his bed. She wasn't complete.

He drew her down some steps and pressed her back against the gated door of a closed laundromat. His hands mapped her body. He knew it. He knew its flaws. It was his to touch. Feeling the thorns in the bouquet pressed between them and drunk from the sweet rose smell, he could tell her need by her disorderly breathing but he refused to fulfill it. "Let's go, my little Marilyn," he whispered. She shuddered as his breath traced the shell curve of her ear and thought of paradise. She didn't ask where they were going. She didn't really care.

"I wish I was in Hawaii," she said.

"I'll take you to Hawaii," said Buddy. He took her to The Agency. The security guard winked as they passed by, Buddy and the disheveled blond. He didn't make them sign the register. He knew Buddy. They talked sports. "Somebody's got to get the blonds," he said to himself as he watched Lucille ooze into the elevator.

Buddy unlocked the Hell room and activated the monitor. He poured Lucille a paper cup full of cool water from the dispenser. She put it to her forehead before she sipped. She watched Buddy straddle an upholstered stool as he pressed buttons without watching where his fingers hit. He stared at the screen, forgot her for several minutes, and then Lucille saw her face. In the dark room, on a television screen, it seemed flat, strange, like someone else's face. "That's me," she said.

Buddy ignored her. He brought a grid up over the image and then, with one finger, he fixed it in the computer's memory. With another, he summoned the face of Marilyn Monroe. "Marilyn." The grid reappeared. "Now you." Lucille's face slid on to the screen from left to right. Using the grid, Buddy manipulated her image until it lay directly over Marilyn Monroe's, matching her ears to Marilyn's ears, her nose to Marilyn's nose, her mouth to Marilyn's mouth, her hairline to Marilyn's hairline. When the sandwiching was as exact as it was going to get, Buddy pressed a button and the grid fell out and away leaving a merged face that belonged to neither Marilyn Monroe nor Lucille. "Now watch," said Buddy. He cupped his hand over a gray electronic mouse and moved in across a dull pad. A blue line appeared at the tip of the merged noses. The blue line outlined Marilyn's nose. Buddy pressed a button and those parts of Lucille's nose that did not fall within the blue line were illuminated in red. "Here's the main thing. To start. We'll have to work on the nose."

"How do we work on the nose?" asked Lucille.

"Let's use our little brains. Now how do you *think* we work on the nose?"

Lucille understood. "You want me to get a nose job?"

"You want to be Marilyn?"

"Yeah, but . . ."

"Don't 'yeah, but,' precious."

"I never even had my tonsils out."

"Even Marilyn had to have a nose job to look like Marilyn," Buddy assured her. He put an arm around her shoulder. "And you barely feel it."

"You ever had a nose job?"

Buddy swirled his seat to face her. His eyes were as flat as the eyes on the screen and his voice turned monotone. "Look, we can quit right now."

Lucille nuzzled into his neck. "You don't have to be crabby."

"All right, then," he answered. He showed her where she would need electrolysis to pull her hairline back to create a higher brow. Since she was squeamish, he didn't mention little needles and electric current. "I'll make the appointments. We'll go together." She'd find out. So what? "I'll hold your hand," he said. "The cheeks are good." There was almost no red between her lines and Marilyn's. "The chin is good. And the mouth . . ." Buddy kissed her mouth, holding his lips against her two Marilyn lips, closing his eyes until he pulled away and glanced back at the screen. ". . . is hers. You want to do more?"

"Kisses? Anytime."

"The body."

"No. Kisses."

Buddy obliged. Enough for now.

When he heard her key in the door, the shoe man wrapped a robe over his T-shirt and shorts and shuffled down the hall to open it. "So." The lipstick had been kissed off her mouth. "A victory celebration?"

"Not exactly," said Lucille. Not unless seeing her imperfections and agreeing to have her nose moved around was a celebration.

"What's wrong?"

"I guess I'm just tired," she said.

The shoe man fixed her a hot cup of camomile tea and sat tenderly beside her as he might have sat beside the child he might have had when the child he might have had came in soaked, shivering and sniffling from the rain. "You did great tonight. No one coulda looked more like Marilyn Monroe except Marilyn Monroe and even she mighta come in second next to you, swear to God."

Lucille began to cry.

"Is it him?"

Lucille shook her head. "No. It's me. I'm not going to sign," she began.

The shoe man didn't understand how, if all she'd wanted was to be a Marilyn model, she had decided—that was how she put it to him, that she herself had decided—not to work for Resemblances.

"I don't want to be just another nobody," she answered.

"Nobody's a nobody," said Jack. "What's a nobody?"

"I don't know," said Lucille.

"Did he call you a nobody? Am I a nobody?" the shoe man persisted. " 'Cause if I am, I'm going to quit paying taxes right here and now."

"You're the most important person in the world," said Lucille, and she kissed him on the forehead. "And I got fifteen hundred casharoony in the bank so tomorrow straight after you close up the shop I'm taking us out to The Steak Place for two filet mignons and baked potatoes."

"And Champagne! On me. To celebrate."

"No, on me."

And so they dickered about who would pay for the Champagne which was a wonderful thing to dicker about, but the important thing is not who bought the brut. The next evening, they ate and drank toasts to each other, to trips to Europe and palm trees in Honolulu and the glorious future ahead and for a few hours there was no Buddy, no thought of a new nose or a higher forehead, and Marilyn Monroe was dead and buried, right where she belonged.

The Death of Marilyn Monroe

Sharon Olds

The ambulance men touched her cold
body, lifted it, heavy as iron,
onto the stretcher, tried to close the
mouth, closed the eyes, tied the
arms to the sides, moved a caught
strand of hair, as if it mattered,
saw the shape of her breasts, flattened by
gravity, under the sheet,
carried her, as if it were she,
down the steps.

These men were never the same. They went out
afterwards, as they always did,
for a drink or two, but they could not meet
each other's eyes.

            Their lives took
a turn—one had nightmares, strange
pains, impotence, depression. One did not
like his work, his wife looked
different, his kids. Even death
seemed different to him—a place where she
would be waiting,

and one found himself standing at night
in the doorway to a room of sleep, listening to a
woman breathing, just an ordinary
woman
breathing.

Contributors

J. G. BALLARD was born in Shanghai in 1930 and was interned by the Japanese from 1942 to 1945, an experience reflected in *Empire of the Sun*. Since the publication of his first novel, *The Drowned World*, in 1961, he has written many provocative works including *The Atrocity Exhibition*, *Crash*, *High-Rise*, *Concrete Island*, *The Unlimited Dream Company*, and *The Day of Creation*.

CLIVE BARKER is a master of contemporary horror. His books include *The Damnation Game*, *Books of Blood Vol. 1–3*, *Age of Desire*, *The Great and Secret Show*, *The Thief of Always: A Fable*, and *Imajica*.

JEANNE BEAUMONT is a free-lance medical editor in New York City. Her poetry has appeared in *Poetry*, *The Nation*, *Gettysburg Review*, and *Boulevard*.

CHARLES BUKOWSKI (1920–1994) was born in Andernach, Germany, the son of a U.S. soldier and a German woman, and grew up in Los Angeles. He published his first story when he was twenty-four and began writing poetry at the age of thirty-five. His forty-five books of poetry and prose garnered him an international reputation. Titles include the screenplay to the movie *Barfly*, *Septuagenarian Stew: Stories & Poems*, *The Roominghouse Madrigals: Early Selected Poems*, *Love Is a Dog from Hell*, *The Last Night of the Earth Poems*, and *Run with the Hunted: a Charles Bukowski Reader*.

PHYLLIS BURKE's novel, *Atomic Candy*, was published by Atlantic Monthly Press in 1989.

SUSAN COMPO's *Life After Death and Other Stories* was published by Faber & Faber in 1990.

ELEANOR E. CROCKETT lives in Austin, Texas, where she shapes booklets out of recycled materials for her Bonton Books imprint. She is the author of *Down on 6th Street* (Snake, Rattle and Roll) and *'53 Ford* (Wings Press).

JULIA P. DUBNER has had short stories in *Bakunin* and the *Painted Hills Review*. She received her M.A. from the University of California—Davis, and now lives and works in New York City.

JUDY GRAHN is a poet and the author of many books including *The Works of a Common Woman*, *Another Mother Tongue*, *The Queen of Wands*, *The Queen of Swords* and *Blood, Bread and Roses*.

NANCI GRIFFITH is a singer-songwriter. Her albums include *Poet In My Window*, *Lone Star State of Mind*, *Storms*, and *Other Voices Other Rooms*.

DORIS GRUMBACH is one of this country's most distinguished novelists and critics. Her novels include *Chamber Music*, *The Missing Person*, *The Ladies*, and *The Magician's Girl*. Two volumes of her memoirs have been published: *Coming Into The End Zone* and *Extra Innings*. She was previously the literary editor of *The New Republic* and has been a regular book reviewer for National Public Radio. She lives in Sargentville, Maine.

MICHAEL HEMMINGSON is 27, lives in San Diego, California, and is the author of *The Naughty Yard*, a novel, and several poetry chapbooks. His play, *Driving Somewhere*, is forthcoming from the West Coast Play Series.

HILLARY JOHNSON is the author of the novel *Physical Culture*. She recently contributed to *The Wild Palms Reader*. She lives in Los Angeles.

MICHAEL LALLY was born in Orange, New Jersey in 1942. Since winning the New York Poetry Center's "Discovery Award" in 1972 and editing the seminal new poetry anthology *None Of The Above*, he has gone on to act in both television and movies. His books include *The South Orange Sonnets*, *Rocky Dies Yellow*, and *Catch My Breath*. He currently lives in Santa Monica, California.

L. A. LANTZ is studying for her Masters in Applied Anthropology at American University in Washington, D.C. She recently received an honorable mention in the Nimrod/Hardman awards for fiction.

LYN LIFSHIN is the author of over eighty books. Recent titles include *Kiss the Skin Off*, *Rubbed Silk*, and *The Doctor Poems*. She has edited a series of books on women's writing: *Tangled Vines*, *Ariadne's Web*, and *Unsealed Lips*. She is also the subject of the documentary *Not Made of Glass*.

BETH MEACHAM is an executive editor at Tor Books.

TAYLOR MEAD grew up in Grosse Pointe, Michigan. The actor-writer is perhaps best known for starring in films like *Hallelujah the Hills*, *The Queen of Sheba Meets the Atom Man*, *The Flower Thief*, *Babo 73*, and Andy Warhol's *Lonesome Cowboys*. His diary has appeared in three volumes, the most recent being *On Amphetamine and in Europe: Excerpts from the Anonymous Diary of a New York Youth*.

BILL MORRIS was born in Washington, D.C., and grew up in Detroit. His novel, *Motor City*, was published in 1992. He lives in North Carolina, where he's a columnist for the *Greensboro News and Record*.

SHARON OLDS was born in 1942, in San Francisco, and educated at Stanford University and Columbia University. Her award winning poetry volumes are *Satan Says*, *The Dead and the Living*, *The Gold Cell*, and *The Father*.

ROBERT PETERS was born in 1924 on a northern Wisconsin farm. He has a Ph.D. in Victorian Literature and taught for years, until his recent retirement, at the University of California—Irvine. A prolific poet, performer, and critic, his works include *Crunching Gravel: Growing Up in the*

Thirties, What Dillinger Meant to Me, Love Poems for Robert Mitchum, A Night with the Undertaker's Grandson, Where the Bee Sucks: Workers, Drones, and *Queens of Contemporary American Poetry.*

LESLIE PIETRZYK lives in Alexandria, Virginia. Her fiction has appeared in *The Iowa Review, Epoch, The Gettysburg Review, North Dakota Quarterly, South Carolina Review,* and many others.

JOHN RECHY, the author of *The Sexual Outlaw,* was born in El Paso, Texas, in 1934. His novels include *City of Night, The Vampires, The Fourth Angel, Rushes, Bodies and Souls,* and *Marilyn's Daughter.* He is on the faculty of the University of Southern California where he teaches creative writing, literature, and film courses.

GREGG SHAPIRO lives in Chicago, where he is a cofounding member of SoPo Writers and coeditor of *Queer Planet Review.* His poetry and fiction have appeared in *Christopher Street, Plum Review, The Washington Blade, Gargoyle,* and *The Quarterly.* He was married on the Supreme Court steps during the National March on Washington for Gay and Lesbian Rights in 1993. A volume of his short stories, *Indiscretion,* is available on disk from Sheridan Square Press.

ROSANNE DARYL THOMAS is a graduate of the Columbia University film school and the author, under the pseudonym Prince Charming, of *Complications.* Her novel *The Angel Carver* was published in 1993. She lives in Ridgefield, Connecticut.

LYNNE TILLMAN was born in New York City, where she now lives. She is the author of three novels, *Haunted Houses, Motion Sickness,* and *Cast in Doubt. Absence Makes the Heart* is her collection of short fiction. She was also the co-director and writer of the feature film *Committed.*

SAM TOPEROFF is the author of *Lost Sundays, Sugar Ray Leonard, All the Advantages,* and *Queen of Desire.* He lives in Huntington, New York, and Champ Clavel, France.

DAVID TRINIDAD is the author of six books of poetry, including *Hand Over Heart, November,* and *Monday, Monday.* His poetry has appeared in *City Lights Review, New American Writing,* and *BOMB.* Originally from Los Angeles, Trinidad now lives in New York City.

RITA VALENCIA lives in Los Angeles. Her work has been included in the M.I.T. "L.A. Hot & Cool" catalog, the Museum of Contemporary Art (L.A.) "Helter Skelter Exhibit" catalog, *Spectacle Magazine, Now Time Magazine,* and *Fiction International.*

TOM WHALEN is the author of *The Eustachia Stories, Elongated Fictions,* and co-author with Michael Presti of *The Camel's Back.* His fiction has appeared in *Sudden Fiction, That's What I Like (About the South): New Southern Stories for the Nineties, Elvis in Oz,* and other anthologies. A graduate of the University of Arkansas and Hollins College, he directs the creative writing program at the New Orleans Center for Creative Arts.